GRAY JUSTICE

ALAN McDERMOTT
GRAY JUSTICE

Text copyright © 2014 Alan McDermott

Published by Thomas & Mercer, Seattle

www.apub.com

Amazon, the Amazon logo, and Thomas & Mercer are trademarks of Amazon.com, Inc., or its affiliates.

ISBN-13: 9781477818497
ISBN-10: 1477818499

5579 8432
9/14

Cover design by The Book Designers

Library of Congress Control Number: 2013920364

Printed in the United States of America

In the back, Tim Garbutt nodded his head to the current beat and voiced his displeasure when the disc was changed.

'Aww, I was listening to that.'

'Stop bleating, Timmy,' Kyle said, switching the CD for something with a bit more drum and bass. 'My gran wouldn't even listen to that crap.'

Boyle laughed, but his eyes were on the black Ford coming towards them. The thick aerial first caught his attention, and as it neared, he saw the white shirts and black epaulettes of the occupants that identified them as police in an unmarked car. The Ford passed them, and in his rear view mirror he watched it continue for another hundred yards before the blue lights illuminated and it performed a U-turn.

Game on.

———⁓———

'That's Stuart Boyle in the Scooby,' PC Trevor Haines told his partner. That was enough for his colleague, Glenn Barker, and he hit the blues and twos before spinning the car around in pursuit.

'Hotel Oscar, this is Romeo Tango Two Five. Can we have a PNC check on a blue Subaru Impreza, licence number Whiskey Victor Five Three Victor Kilo Mike.'

Although it was procedure to check the Police National Computer, the call in was a formality. PC Haines knew for a fact that Stuart Boyle didn't own a Subaru Impreza, nor could he have insurance to drive one because he didn't have a driving licence. In fact, Stuart Boyle had never had a valid licence: his driving ban started before he was even old enough to apply for one, and he had a string of motoring convictions, ranging from driving without a licence, driving whilst disqualified and driving without insurance, theft of a motor vehicle and taking without the owner's consent. All this despite being just twenty years of age.

I would like to thank my family for putting up with me during the time it took to write this story.

Prologue

21 January 2010

Stuart Boyle held the Subaru Impreza at a steady thirty miles p[er]
hour as he headed towards the town centre. Red traffic lights hal[t]
his progress, and he gazed around at the people in the cars, on
buses, walking the streets, or sitting in their offices, most of t[hem]
either at work or heading to work.

He couldn't understand the appeal of working eight h[ours]
doing someone else's bidding all day long for a just a cou[ple of]
hundred pounds a week. In comparison, he was sitting in [a]
motor that took just three minutes to steal and would earn [a]
hundred pounds by the end of the day. The fact that he r[isked]
got caught didn't bother him: it was an occupational ris[k he was]
willing to take. Capture was simply an inconvenience[, a]
few hours spent in a cell when he could be out casing h[is]

No, as things stood, work wasn't for him.

He caressed the wheel of the Subaru he had stol[en]
before, wishing he could keep it a bit longer, but he'd [told]
Sammy Christodoulou that he had it. Sammy want[ed it]
away, and you didn't piss around with Sammy. No, [hand it]
over, take the cash and see what tomorrow brings. M[aybe keep]
the next one to himself for a few days.

'See what other music they got,' he ordered M[att, who]
was sitting in the passenger seat.

'Romeo Tango Two Five, this is Hotel Oscar. The vehicle is registered to a Mr Simon Glover, Winslow Way, Meopham, Kent. It was reported stolen at eight this morning.'

'Romeo Tango Two Five, roger that. We believe the driver is a Stuart Boyle, currently disqualified from driving. We are three hundred yards behind it, heading north on Hall Lane, over.'

'He's seen us,' Haines told his colleague.

'Looks like it. Fasten your seat belt, 'cause he ain't one for pulling over,' Barker advised. Sure enough, the Subaru was soon doing sixty miles per hour, and their Ford was keeping up, but not gaining.

'Hotel Oscar, Romeo Tango Two Five, vehicle failing to stop, continuing west, speed six zero miles an hour. Traffic is light, visibility is excellent, weather is clear, driver is pursuit trained, over.'

As soon as the blue lights illuminated, Stuart was plotting his course home. Once in the network of streets on the Foxwell estate, he was confident he could lose them. It was just a case of getting there before they managed to stop him. At this time of day, the ring road was the quickest way back, especially in an Impreza.

He hit the accelerator and was soon doing sixty through the morning traffic, weaving between cars and speeding down the centre of the road, forcing other drivers onto the kerb. At the traffic lights he was held up by stationary cars, so he took to the oncoming lane and sped through the junction, narrowly avoiding a collision with a bus coming from his right.

The move held the police up, and he gained an advantage, pulling a further hundred yards ahead, but another set of red traffic lights evened things out, and he had to slow in order to squeeze into a gap between a car and a van. The police were right on his tail now, and traffic ahead was stopped, so he took to the pavement, scattering pedestrians as he searched desperately for a clear stretch of road. Up ahead he saw nothing but stationary vehicles, so he turned into a side road and sped along residential streets at twice the speed limit.

He checked his rear view mirror as he took another turn and saw the police car in the distance, and he guessed he had enough of an advantage, just as long as he could maintain it. Another right turn and he was back on the main road, with the ring road only a few hundred yards ahead.

'Hotel Oscar, Romeo Tango Two Five, vehicle has joined the ring road, heading west, speed now eight zero miles an hour.' PC Haines gave the commentary while PC Barker concentrated on the driving.

'Understood, Two Five.'

The pursuit carried on for two miles with no sign of the Subaru slowing down. If anything, it was pulling away from the Ford.

'Hotel Oscar, Romeo Tango Two Five, we believe he may be heading for the Foxwell estate. Do we have any other units in that area, over?' Haines asked. If they didn't get the Scooby contained soon, they were sure to lose them, even if they knew who was at the wheel. Recognising Stuart Boyle was one thing, but having proof that he was ever in the car was another matter entirely. He was too clever to touch a car without surgical gloves, and his family would provide a watertight alibi, as always. No, their only chance was to catch him at the wheel.

'Romeo Tango Two Five, we have no units available at the moment, and Quebec Hotel Nine Nine is on another call, over.'

Damn! QH99, the force helicopter, would have been invaluable in this pursuit, especially if they lost sight of the vehicle and the suspects decamped.

Boyle pulled off the dual carriageway a mile from his home, and although it felt like he had slowed considerably, he was still travelling at seventy miles per hour through the light traffic. Behind him the unmarked car was closing, but he had enough of a lead as he turned into the estate. He told Martin to turn the music off and took the first left, then a right and a left again, and with the windows open he could hear the sirens disappearing in the opposite direction. He still wasn't out of the woods, though. He was well known among the local constabulary, and there was a chance that they might have recognised him. They would also have the chopper up searching for the car, he was sure of that. He had to get home as soon as possible so that his family could swear that he had been in the house all along.

He took the next right into a cul-de-sac, stopped the car and was out and running in no time. His passengers were moments behind him, and all three headed for an alley which led to Alba Street and Boyle's house. Had any of them looked back, they would have seen the Subaru rolling gently down the slight incline of the street. Slowly at first, but the momentum soon built up and it gathered pace all the time ...

Dina Gray stood outside her sister's door, saying her goodbyes after discussing the upcoming birthday party. Daniel made his way up the garden steps and out into the street, where he looked over the low wall into Sarah's garden and started singing 'Ten Green Bottles'.

Dina looked up at her son, marvelling at how quickly he had picked up that song. He'd only heard it for the first time at the beginning of the week, and here he was counting down from ten to zero. It was hard to believe that he would be three years old at the weekend: it seemed like just yesterday that he was learning to crawl. Now he could count, he knew the alphabet, he could read a dozen words and loved to sing. She knew he would have lots of fun in the soft play area of the local activity centre next weekend, and she was also looking forward to it immensely.

'I really envy you,' Sarah said. 'I wish I could get my lazy sod of a husband off the beer long enough to get it up, then I might stand a chance of having another little darling like him.'

Sarah's own kids were all grown up, and she felt broody every time Daniel popped round, but that didn't stop her volunteering to babysit at every opportunity.

With the front of the garden being elevated, neither Dina nor Sarah saw the Subaru until it was a few feet away. There was barely time to recognise the danger before it hit the wall at only twelve miles per hour. When it hit, it wasn't going quite fast enough to demolish the wall, but fast enough to crush the life out of Daniel Gray.

Chapter One

28 October 2010

The alarm clock heralded the start of a new day, and it came as some relief to Tom Gray, rousing him from yet another nightmare.

In the months since Daniel had been gone, he had rarely been able to sleep without dreaming of the incident. At first he had thought it a blessing that he hadn't witnessed Daniel's death, so he could remember his son as he was the last time he saw him alive, but as the weeks went on he found that each dream saw Daniel dying in more bizarre and painful ways. In all of these dreams he was there, watching it all unfold, but helpless to do anything about it.

The relief soon turned to anguish, though, as he remembered what the day had in store.

As much as Daniel's death had hurt him, he had been able to immerse himself in his work. For his wife there had been no such distraction. She had shunned friends and sat alone in the house day after day, hitting the bottle. He had lost count of the number of times he had arrived home to find her drunk and watching a home movie: Daniel learning to eat with a spoon, Daniel taking his first steps, Daniel saying 'Daddy' for the first time ...

Every evening was spent consoling her, urging her to get back in touch with her friends and carry on with life, and despite her promises that she would, he saw little evidence of things improving.

The fact that he hadn't spotted the signs for what they were would haunt Tom Gray for the rest of his days, but today more than any other.

It was time to have a shower, shave and head to the office to do the payroll.

In the afternoon he would bury his wife.

Stopping only at a sandwich bar to grab a bacon roll, Gray drove to the offices of Viking Security Services and filled his parking space near the front door. He had started this company a few months after leaving the army and had been supplying security personnel to domestic and foreign companies for the last five years. His main income came from supplying BGs, or bodyguards, to companies operating in regions affected by the recent upheaval in the Gulf states, although he also provided staff specialising in training private defence teams. His first such contract was supplying advisors to a Saudi prince to train his personal guard, and the job they had done had cemented his reputation. Gray currently had a team of five permanent advisors, plus over one hundred other freelance staff on his books, ready to take a job at a moment's notice, half of whom were already in the field. Each of them was earning Viking Security Services a commission of one hundred pounds a day.

All of the people he employed were either personally selected, having served with them, or came highly recommended by former colleagues still in the forces. If a soldier cut the mustard in his old regiment, he would be pointed in Gray's direction when he left. His insistence on selecting only the best in their field made him the standout choice for close protection contracts.

He got out of his BMW convertible after putting the roof up to protect the interior from the seagulls that mobbed the area. One of the local residents liked to feed these birds each morning, which meant at least thirty of them would be on the wing, screaming past his office window and shitting all over his car. He wouldn't have minded if they had been little sparrows or blue tits, but seagulls were nothing more than flying rats. They nested on buildings, they ate garbage—often destroying the garbage bag and spreading its contents all over the street in the process—and they made such a racket whenever a rival ventured to within fifty yards of their territory. Perhaps one day they would abandon the city and return to the sea, but as long as this ignorant cow kept inviting them for breakfast, Tom wasn't going to hold his breath.

Inside the office building Tom stopped off at the kitchen to get a coffee to go with his sandwich. He ate after mating the laptop with the docking station on his desk, and once it had powered up, he went for a quick look at the BBC News website. The intention was to get the World News section to check on developments in Syria, where he had a team of seven contractors, but before he could navigate to the page the main headline caught his eye:

'*Anger at killer driver's sentence*'

Gray clicked the link and read the article, which told of a seventeen-year-old youth who received a five-hundred-pound fine and a twelve-month driving ban for killing his passenger girlfriend when he crashed his car. He had admitted driving without due care and attention rather than face the charge of causing death by dangerous driving.

He thought about Stuart Boyle, the man who had killed Daniel. The police wouldn't give Gray any specific details about Boyle due to the trial, which was starting today, but one officer had admitted he had 'previous'. They were confident of a conviction, and the fact that Boyle had been remanded in custody at the start of the year suggested their case was good. They had CCTV evidence of Boyle leaving the driver's side door, which was captured by a resident who had installed the cameras after being plagued by the local youths.

Gray would miss the first day of Boyle's trial, which was expected to last all week, but would be in court for the remaining days and the verdict.

Another headline caught his eye:

'M1 closed near Luton after crash kills two'

His thoughts immediately turned to his wife. The coroner's verdict was suicide based on the fact that she had removed her seat belt and disabled the air bag before ploughing into the motorway bridge support at over 110 miles per hour. Gray didn't dispute their decision, but since her death he had cursed himself daily for not realising she wasn't as strong as him, and he knew he should have seen the signs. His army training had taught him that death inevitably came for everyone, and when you lose someone close, you celebrate their life, not mourn their passing.

On this day, that training abandoned him, and he cried like he hadn't cried in his thirty-six years.

The funeral was held at the same church where their son was laid to rest. The mourners were equally split between Dina's family and Gray's ex-army friends, separated by the coffin suspended over the hole in the ground.

Tom's parents had handed him to social services as a toddler, and he had been raised by foster family after foster family until he was old enough to join the army and finally find people with whom he could truly bond. They were his only family now.

To Gray, the service seemed to be over as soon as it had started. He had spent the entire time in his own recollections and heard few of the words spoken by the vicar, not even allowing the late autumn drizzle to penetrate his little world.

Eventually a hand on his shoulder brought him back to the present, and he saw that the coffin had already been lowered into the ground. He stood confused for a moment, not knowing if he should throw some soil on the coffin or say a few words, but thankfully everyone opposite turned to leave and he took that as a cue to do the same. He moved to catch up with Dina's mother, but his wife's brother stopped and put up his hand. 'Now is not the time, Tom.'

Tom Gray had a feeling there would never be a right time, because Ruth had made it plain that she blamed him for Dina's death. He had phoned numerous times, but Ruth never took or returned his calls. Eventually he had driven to the house to confront her, only to be told that she didn't want to see him. 'Mum's taken it hard,' Dina's brother had told him. 'How could you let Dina get into that state? Didn't you notice something was wrong?'

Gray had offered him no answers and had left without making his peace. That had been his last contact with Dina's family, and now it seemed there would be no more.

'Come on, Tom, let's grab a drink.'

Len Smart led Gray to his car, and they drove in silence to the pub. Once inside, with pints in front of them, Gray said, 'I should go to the wake, Len.'

'No, Tom, you shouldn't. Give them time. They'll come round, but right now let them grieve.'

'I guess you're right.'

A dozen of Gray's friends walked into the pub, having followed them from the church. Two headed to the bar to get a round in, while the rest pulled tables around so that they were all sitting together.

'How's the business coming along?' Carl Levine asked, although he already knew the answer: he just wanted a topic to take Gray's mind off the day's proceedings.

'Not too bad. I got a contract for three BGs in Afghanistan last week, and another coming up for eight in Iraq, looking after oil workers. I'll be meeting with the oil company in a couple of weeks.'

'Sounds good. When you get it, don't forget your old friend Len.'

'Don't worry,' Gray assured him. 'When the contract's signed, you'll be second on the list.'

Len appeared hurt. 'Only second? Who's first? Not Sonny, surely.'

Simon 'Sonny' Baines was so named because he'd looked like a schoolboy when he'd enlisted and hadn't seemed to age a day since. Along with his youthful looks, he had a penchant for school-boy pranks, many of which were at Len's expense.

'No, not Sonny. Me.'

'But what about the business? What happens to that when you're running around Baghdad?'

Gray took a mouthful of beer. 'It's up for sale. One venture capitalist firm has already shown interest. We haven't discussed numbers yet, but my accountant reckons I should be looking for about one point eight million.'

'This is a bit sudden. What brought it on?' Jeff Campbell asked.

Gray took another long drink, keeping them all waiting. He had known these men for many years, and they had been through a lot together, yet he still felt uncomfortable opening up in front of them. They had shared many things in their time, but rarely their emotions.

'I just can't bear it without them,' he finally said, staring into his glass. 'If I stay around here it will drive me crazy, I know it. When Dina and Danny were both alive, I would think about them on the drive home, and every time I opened the door he would run to me shouting, "Daddy"! Now, when I open the door, there's just silence, and it tears me apart.'

His eyes began to cloud, and he wiped them before finishing off his beer. As he put his empty glass on the table, it was immediately replaced with a fresh pint.

'Whenever I pass his nursery, I think of him. When I go to the supermarket, I remember the times we used to go as a family, and I even sleep on the couch because I can't stand to be alone in our bed. When I see a woman and kid in the street, it reminds me of them.

'There are just too many things in my daily routine that make me think about my family. I need a fresh start, get out of the area and throw myself into something that will take up every waking moment. The only thing I know that intense is a stint in Iraq.'

'But why sell up?' Colin Avery asked. 'Couldn't you just get a manager in for a while?'

'I could,' Gray admitted, 'but I want a clean slate. I don't want to come back to the old routine; it'll just bring back the memories. This way, once I'm done in Iraq, I can settle anywhere I like.' A few nods told him that they thought his plan made sense.

A couple of them asked about positions in the upcoming contract, and he began taking the names, but was interrupted when his mobile rang. The display told him it was his solicitor, so he made his excuses and moved to a quieter area of the room. He listened for a few moments, then suddenly exploded into the phone: 'You're fucking joking!'

Everyone at the table looked at him, their eyes asking what the problem was. Gray listened for another minute or so before ending the call and resuming his seat at the table.

'They released him,' he told his friends, and knocked back a whiskey which was sitting in the middle of the table. 'Apparently he offered to plead guilty if they changed the charge to driving without due care and attention. The prosecution accepted the offer, and the judge gave him fifteen months, and then released him because he had already served more than half of that on remand.'

'Why only fifteen months?' Paul Bennett asked. 'Was it his first offence?'

'Fuck, no.' Gray spat. 'My solicitor said he had forty-three previous convictions for car theft, plus thirty-four other convictions including assault, burglary, possessing an offensive weapon and various drug offences.'

'So that's it? He just walks?'

'He just walks,' Gray confirmed.

'He's just spent eight months with his own kind, learning new and improved ways of breaking into cars, and now he's free to try them out,' Sonny said. 'That can't be right.'

'This country's too soft on these little shits,' Tristram Barker-Fink agreed.

'They should bring back National Service, give them some real discipline.'

' ... or the birch ... '

Other suggestions came thick and fast, including 'chop their thieving hands off' and 'just shoot them in the fucking head.'

'Want us to pay him a visit?' Avery asked, and a few of them nodded their willingness to take part.

'Thanks, guys,' Gray said, a faraway look in his eye, 'but I think it's gone beyond that now ... '

Chapter Two

12 April 2011

Joseph Olemwu desperately wanted some gear, but with no cash he would have to find a different form of currency. Luckily, Albert Tonga accepted mobile phones as full payment, and at this time of night there was always the chance of finding someone to donate one, even if they didn't do so willingly.

He took a large swig of vodka and passed the bottle to Vinnie Parker. 'Robbo told me he did it with Shelly White on Friday,' Parker told him before wiping the neck of the bottle and taking a drink. Olemwu nearly choked with laughter, vodka erupting from his nose and clenched mouth.

When he finally recovered he said, 'Robbo is full of shit. He didn't shag no one on Friday. I was drinking with him all day, and the last I saw him, he was puking in the stairwell at midnight. I had to help him to his flat. Fuck me, his mum was pissed off.' He smiled at the recollection and imagined the bollocking that would have been dished out.

Marcus Taylor tapped Olemwu and Parker on the arm and motioned towards a figure approaching them. He was at least six inches smaller than any of the boys, perhaps a couple of years older than them at around twenty years of age, wearing glasses and hair cut short with a side parting. He was chatting on a mobile, seemingly oblivious to their presence until he was on top of them.

The man stopped when he noticed the three boys and made eye contact for a brief moment, then haltingly walked on past them, keeping them in his peripheral vision.

Olemwu was the first to react. 'What the fuck are you looking at?'

The man carried on walking, his pace quickening, and the boys trotted to catch up. As they got within ten feet of him, he took off through a gate and into the park. The three boys followed, chasing him into the darkness. He had on a light-brown jacket and that helped them keep him in view, but they didn't seem to be gaining. As they ran three abreast, the two on the flanks were suddenly confronted by figures dressed entirely in black, who seemed to rise out of the ground barely five feet in front of them. Their momentum carried them towards the men, who took a step to the side and swung baseball bats, catching the boys in the chest. Ribs cracked and they dropped likes sacks of cement.

Neither had managed to get out a cry, but Olemwu had heard the bats striking, as had the man he was chasing. Both stopped, and the man in the brown jacket turned and started walking purposefully towards him, placing his glasses in a protective case. Despite the height advantage, there was something menacing in the slight figure that deeply troubled him. He spun round to seek strength in numbers, but from the faint street lighting he saw his friends lying in the foetal position, barely able to moan, never mind move. From the sides two dark figures approached him, leaving him nowhere to run.

'Look man, I don't want no trouble. We was just fuckin' wiv 'im, that's all.'

The men said nothing, simply moved closer and closer, bats raised and ready to strike. Joseph Olemwu's head spun as he tried to keep an eye on all of them at the same time, and when the blow came, he barely saw the blur of the wood before it crashed into his temple. He dropped to the ground, out cold, and the men wasted no time applying plasticuffs to his arms and legs. Sonny Baines put his glasses case back in his jacket pocket and clicked the talk button on his collar mike twice. The three men picked the unconscious Olemwu up and carried him into the darkness, and after a hundred yards Sonny heard a voice in his earpiece. 'Seventy yards out, eleven o'clock.' Sonny adjusted his heading and saw the transit van when he was within ten yards of it. The driver was scanning the surrounding area with night vision glasses, ensuring there was no one around to disturb them. Satisfied, he opened the rear doors, and Olemwu was bundled in unceremoniously.

'Christ, Carl, could you have hit him any harder? You nearly took his fucking head off.'

'He's fine, look,' Carl said, giving Olemwu a kick. 'He's breathing, ain't he?'

The van pulled out of the park, and once on the road the driver turned the headlights on. In the back they settled down for the long journey, using Joseph Olemwu as a footrest.

Chapter Three

Sunday, 17 April 2011

John Hammond was preparing his notes for the next morning's Joint Intelligence Committee meeting when Andrew Harvey knocked on his door and walked in without waiting to be beckoned. Normally Hammond would have had something to say about the intrusion, but Harvey was a solid operative, very experienced and above all a man who knew when to stand on convention. If he ignored the unwritten protocol, it was often with good reason.

'Something big has come in,' Harvey told him. 'We're all gathered.'

Hammond nodded, locked his workstation and followed Harvey. In the conference room, Diane Lane used their arrival as her cue to start the briefing.

'In the last thirty minutes, calls were made to all the major newspapers as well as the BBC and Sky News channels to inform them about this new website.'

She pressed her remote control and an image of the website appeared on the fifty-inch, wall-mounted, plasma screen. The banner proclaimed the site to be the home of 'Justice For Britain' and in the centre of the page a video was waiting to be streamed. Lane clicked 'Play' on the embedded video player, and a man appeared on the screen, not overly handsome, the mouth perhaps a little small, but the face under the short chestnut hair had an air of authority. He moved the camera so that it was pointing towards what appeared to be five prison cells, all with their doors open. Each cell contained a single boxlike chair upon which sat a shaven-headed figure wearing a white T-shirt and nothing else. They all had tape over their mouths, and their arms were outstretched and tied to the cell walls, while their feet were shackled, the chains running through metal rings set into the floor between their legs.

'You are all here,' the man began, walking past the cells and addressing the occupants, 'because you all have criminal records stretching back years. Despite the courts being lenient with you, you have spurned numerous chances to change your ways. You might have thought that the courts were doing you a favour by just giving you a curfew or community service, but it's quite the opposite: if you had committed one crime and learned your lesson, you wouldn't be here. The fact that you have a string of convictions means you have no regard for the law or the people you have plagued over the years. You have shown that you do not want to make a positive contribution to society, and up until now society has had no say in the matter. We have all had to rely on our government to protect us from you, yet they have thrown you back on the street time after time.

'Well, enough is enough. I think you have had all the chances you deserve. I say it is now up to the people of this country to decide what happens to you.'

The figure turned to the camera.

'Folks, my name is Tom Gray and the next few days are all about choices.

'Last year, one of these criminals killed my only son, and our fabulous judicial system gave him a fifteen-month prison sentence and then let him walk free because he had served eight months on remand.

'That was all they thought my son's life was worth.'

Gray took a swig of water from a bottle.

'I have created this website so that you, the people of Britain, can have a say in what happens to these five people. Judges throw them back on the streets because the crimes they commit do not directly affect them. If they did, you can be sure the sentences would be harsher. If a judge's son was killed by a joy rider, you can be sure he would go down for a long time.

'I've contacted all the major UK news outlets to let them know that I have placed a device at a strategic location, and it's capable of killing thousands. If one of my colleagues out there lets me know that this website was interrupted for any reason, I will kill everyone in this room and take my own life, and the device goes off at midday on Friday. I am the only one who knows where the device is, and its location will die with me.'

Gray started to count off on his fingers. 'If the government interfere with this website or cause it to stop functioning, I will take my own life.

'If this story isn't shown on all UK news channels, and that includes showing the address of the website, I will take my own life.

'If any attempt is made to rescue these criminals by force, I will take my own life.'

Gray unzipped his combat smock to reveal a waistcoat fashioned from webbing. Strung from it were three hand grenades, with a cord attached to the pin of the one in the centre. The cord emerged through the lapel of his smock and was attached to a large handle, making it easy to grab.

'In my line of work I have long accepted the fact that death will come, so I do not fear it.

'As the TV and newspapers will no doubt tell you over the coming days and weeks, I spent fourteen years in the army. My knowledge of explosives is more than enough to create and prime the device I mentioned, so do not doubt its existence.'

Gray pulled a photo from his combat smock pocket and studied it for a moment before showing it to the camera.

'Seven months after our son died, my wife took her own life, so I have no more family. The choice I had to make was to either live my life in constant mourning or end it this week while trying to make a difference.

'As you can see, I have made my choice.'

He replaced the photo of his family in his breast pocket and buttoned it up.

'I want to remind the prime minister that his government came to power on the promise to get tough on criminals. Well, now it's time for him to make his choice: Let the public watch these transmissions through to their conclusion on Thursday night, and save the lives of thousands; or try to save these five career criminals.'

Gray made a weighing motion with his hands. 'Thousands of lives or five criminals. All I ask is that you let me finish this, let the country decide the fate of these criminals. Consider it the ultimate straw poll.

'To you out there in Britain, the voting starts now. On the left-hand side of the screen, you will see the profiles and criminal records of the five men here. The first person to be dealt with will be Simon Arkin, aged twenty-one, from Manchester. Simon has sixty-seven convictions but has never been behind bars. Instead, the courts gave him community service, which he hasn't carried out.

'If you think he should be set free to commit more crimes, send an email to tom@justiceforbritain.co.uk. Put the word "Simon" as the subject and the word "Live" in the body of the email. If you think he has had all the chances a person deserves, replace "Live" with "Die". Well, do you think he deserves another chance? I know what I think, but what do *you* think?

'Voting closes at seven thirty this evening, and I will be back with a live broadcast an hour later to reveal the results.'

The video ended and Lane turned to her colleagues after replacing the image of the website with a photo of Tom Gray.

'This image was sent to us by the MoD. They confirm that Tom Gray was one of theirs, but he appears to have understated his role.' After glancing at her notes, she continued. 'He joined Two Para at aged eighteen, and after achieving the rank of sergeant, he joined Two-Two Regiment, where he spent his last eight years, including three tours in Iraq which earned him the Distinguished Conduct Medal. We'll have more details when his file arrives.'

'He's SAS?' Hammond asked.

'It appears so.'

'Which means he probably *will* have the knowhow to create the device he mentioned, so we proceed on that assumption.' Hammond massaged his cheeks for a moment. 'He mentioned colleagues on the outside. Work that up, and see who he has been in contact with over the last six months. Phone records, email account—we need names and addresses for everyone.' The assistant director general of MI5 turned to Harvey. 'Andrew, our main priority is that bomb: Get every available resource looking for it. Once that's rolling, ask the techies to get working on that website. Examine every avenue, and give us some options. I don't want them to make a move—just options.'

The intelligence officer nodded and left the room.

'Diane, I want reports on each of these boys, and get on to GCHQ and surveillance, see if we can find Gray's location. The techies might get us something, but I want to double up on everything.'

Lane nodded and walked towards the door. 'Will do.'

Hammond returned to his office and made a quick phone call before grabbing his briefcase and walking towards the exit. 'I'm going to see the home secretary,' he told Harvey in passing. 'Keep me posted on developments.'

Chapter Four

Tom Gray watched the counter on his laptop as it crept towards two hundred. The freelance programmer who had created the bespoke software had explained that when a new visitor arrived at the website, the Global.asax file captured their IP address and other items in the ServerVariables collection, wrapped them in an XML message and emailed it to his inbox. His email software then dumped it in a folder which was monitored by a FileSystemWatcher component, which extracted the information and fed it into a web service that returned known information based on the server variables and then fed it into a database and displayed the results on the screen, which was refreshed every few seconds by a Timer component.

In layman's terms, if someone visited the website, Gray would know about it and have a good idea who and where they were.

Gray had contacted the news outlets forty minutes earlier, and as no one else in the world knew about the website, he thought it safe to assume that the first visitors would be the news outlets, the government and the intelligence service.

He flicked back and forth between the BBC News and Sky News until he saw the first of the 'Breaking News' tickers scrolling across the bottom of the screen. Gray checked his watch and saw that his prediction was out by three minutes, which was no big deal. It simply meant he would record more IP addresses than anticipated. If the security services hadn't visited by now, they never would.

With the IP addresses recorded, he would now be able to filter out any votes coming from the same range. In considering possible ploys against him, he had reasoned that the authorities might send a few million emails with the word 'Live' in order to rig the vote, but his software would disregard any votes coming from the recorded IP addresses or any with a certain range. In addition, with the click of a button he could redirect any requests for his website from these IP addresses to any other page on the Internet. His choice had been to redirect them to a page on the number10.gov.uk petitions website which was asking the government to reintroduce the death penalty.

Gray also considered the fact that they might try a few ways to influence the results, but this had also been factored in when he had commissioned the software.

He settled down to watch the news, wondering how long it would take them to brand him a terrorist. He didn't have to wait long.

'News is just reaching us that a former SAS soldier is threatening to kill thousands of people unless the government allow him to execute five suspected criminals live on the Internet.'

A photo of Gray appeared on the screen next to the female anchor, a picture he recognised from his army days.

'Tom Gray, who spent eight years in two-two Regiment, Special Air Service, has demanded that the government allow him to poll the nation to decide whether or not his captives should live or die. According to a video shown on his website, www.justiceforbritain. co.uk, if the government do not allow him to collect and act on the votes sent in by members of the public, he will kill his prisoners and take his own life. If he does this, police will have little or no chance of finding his bomb.'

The camera angle changed to show a live video feed on the studio wall. A grey-haired man in his fifties, with heavy jowls and a ruddy complexion, waited patiently for his introduction.

'We are joined now by Home Office spokesman, Adrian Goode. Mr Goode, thank you for joining us. What is the Home Office's response to this terrorist threat?'

Gray watched the spokesman spend four minutes talking a lot but saying absolutely nothing, promising that the government were doing everything within their power to protect the public, while giving no indication as to how it would do this. Questions were thrown at him, and he answered with prepared statements, never once deviating from the script. It was just what Gray had expected.

He turned his attention to his laptop and waited for the votes to start coming in.

———— ∽ ————

Andrew Harvey walked into the Technical Operations office and made his way straight to Gerald Small's workstation.

'What have we got?' he asked.

Small continued tapping at his keyboard as he explained their progress. 'We have the website host. It's a UK company based in Guildford, and he's either too dumb to know how to hide its location, or he doesn't care.'

'Or maybe he wants us to find it,' Harvey suggested. 'What else?'

'We have gained access to the website's source code. It's written in a programming language I am familiar with, and so far I have discovered a couple of interesting bits of code.' Small brought up the first page of interest. 'This area here checks to see if it is operating within a date and time range. That range was a couple of minutes before the first call to the BBC and ended forty-five minutes later. It has collected details of every visitor during that time and sent the details to Gray's email address. What he has done with that information, we don't know, but he wanted it for a reason.'

'Which means he knows our IP address and can block or monitor our visits?'

Small nodded.

'What about using a different terminal?' Harvey asked.

'We access the outside world via a proxy server, so no matter which terminal you use, it will always show the IP address of the proxy. What we can do is use a different connection.' He shuffled his chair to another terminal and opened up a command prompt. After typing for a few moments he declared the job done.

'This terminal uses our failover connection and doesn't use a proxy. It will show up as a residential account if he ever digs that deep.'

'Excellent,' Harvey said. 'So we have anonymous access. What options do we have now?'

Small shuffled back to his own terminal and brought up another page of code.

'This function calls a web service that brings back the results of the votes.' Noticing the blank look from Harvey, he dumbed it down. 'A web service is a way for two websites to talk to each other. The results are going to another server in South Africa, one we don't have access to. This code here calls that other website and asks it to send the results. This means that if we want to manipulate the results, we could do it here, as the results come back. We could easily add 30 percent to the number of "Die" votes and show this as the number of "Live" votes. That way, none of them are killed.'

Harvey looked sceptical. 'I'm worried that he is making this too easy for us. What other options are there?'

'Well,' Small said, rubbing the back of his neck, 'we could intercept all emails going to his inbox and delete every third one that says "Die" before he receives it, I suppose.'

Harvey thought about it for a moment. 'Okay, that's plan A. Let me know if you come up with anything else.' He returned to his own desk and called Hammond to pass on the news.

John Hammond was ushered into the home secretary's office and took the seat offered by the minister. The late spring sun hit him square in the face as he sat down, and he had to lean to his left to avoid its glare and be able to see Stephen Wells. Hammond was sure the chair had been strategically positioned prior to his arrival.

'John, the PM isn't happy that this has been sprung upon him, especially with a general election just six weeks away. He wants to know what we are doing about it.' Hammond's relationship with Wells had been a long and fractured one, and he knew that if things went badly there would be no "we". Even if things went their way, it would be the home secretary who took all the plaudits, while MI5 would get a brief mention if they were lucky.

'Minister, we have our best resources working on it. As we see it, the priority is locating the device he mentioned. Without that, we cannot make a move on him.'

'Do you know where he is?' the home secretary asked.

'Not yet. As I said, our priority is locating the device. There is little point in finding Gray and his captives if we can't make a move on him, so while we have a few people searching for his location, our best efforts are concentrating on possible civilian targets. He claims to be targeting thousands of lives, so that narrows it down a bit. We are concentrating on venues that will have large visitor numbers at midday on Friday, and we are in contact with local police forces who are searching all possible targets.'

'Do you think this man is capable of killing thousands of innocent people?'

'Does he know how to create a device capable of killing thousands? Possibly. I'd even go as far as to say probably. Does he have the resolve to detonate it? That's another matter.'

Wells leaned forward onto his desk and clasped his hands together. 'John, I don't have to tell you how serious it would be if this maniac executes a young man live on the Internet, criminal or not.' He glanced at his watch. 'It's just after midday, giving you seven and a half hours to stop this happening. Find Gray, find his bomb—do whatever you need to do, but put a stop to this, and without loss of life, if you don't mind.'

'We may have more time than that.' Hammond told him. 'On the way over here I spoke to my team. Our techies have access to his website, and we have identified a couple of ways to manipulate his figures. If we can swing the vote our way, we might be able to save the life of the first one.'

'Might?'

'If he has checks in place to ensure we don't tamper with the site, he will spot us messing with the results, but my team is confident that they can intercept negative votes before they hit his system.'

'How confident?'

'There are no guarantees, if that's what you mean, but the alternative is to just let the votes come in and hope the people of Britain have utter faith in the justice system.'

Wells stared at him for a moment, then said, 'Do it.'

Chapter Five

Hamad Farsi placed two thick files on Andrew Harvey's desk and waited for him to finish his phone call.

'Gray?' Harvey asked after hanging up.

Farsi nodded. 'The top one's his MoD jacket, and the other is what we have on him. Nothing much until six months ago, then it all kicks off. Sells his business for just over a million, cash, when it was worth twice as much. He also sold his house for fifty grand under the asking price, obviously looking for a quick sale. Again, it was a cash transaction. After that he went on a spending spree.'

Farsi flicked through the file and pointed out Gray's current account balance.

'Only three thousand left? What the hell did he spend it on?'

'Good question,' Farsi said. 'We have payments to his web-hosting company for a dedicated web server and email exchange server, plus a wire transfer for fifty thousand to a software company in South Africa. There's a hundred and eighty grand to a security firm in Hounslow, and apart from twenty thousand to a software contractor here in London, the rest of the withdrawals were in cash.'

'Have you managed to track down the contractor?' Harvey asked.

'He contacted us. Or should I say, he called the police. He recognised his website and apparently didn't know what he was signing up for. I'm going over there in ten minutes. What do you think Gray did with the rest of the cash?'

'Well, a million quid will get you a nice amount of C4, if you know the right people. And in his line of work, he will probably know the right people. Speaking of which, where's the list of acquaintances?'

'Towards the front of the file. We have a list of the people he recruited through his company, and Diane is compiling a condensed version based on his phone and email records over the last sixty days.'

Harvey skimmed through the file until he came across the mobile phone records. He dialled the number of Gray's phone, and he got a response after two rings. 'Hello?'

'Is this Tom Gray?' he asked.

'Speaking ... '

Harvey put his hand over the receiver and mouthed, 'It's him.'

'My name is Andrew Harvey, calling from Thames House.'

'Hello, Andrew. I expected you to call a lot sooner than this. Call me back on my other phone after two minutes.' He gave Harvey the new number and broke the connection. Too many people knew this number, or knew how to get it, and he didn't want interruptions all day long. He switched sim cards and put the old one in his pocket. Ninety seconds later the phone rang again.

'So, what's this all about, Mr Gray?'

Harvey handed the Post-It note containing the new number to Farsi, who nodded and took it over to Lane's desk so that she could contact her liaison at GCHQ. Their communications capabilities far outstripped those of Thames House, and it wouldn't be long before they could get a location from the number.

'Call me Tom. And what it's about is justice for British people, doing what the government have been promising for twenty years now: protecting the innocent and punishing criminals.'

'We have a judicial system to take care of that, Tom. What you are doing is not going to change anything.'

'Yes, it will,' Gray told him. 'The government have a duty to listen to the people. I am just making sure they hear what is being said.'

'Tom, people have tried for years to change things using terror tactics, and it hasn't worked. You should know—you used to be on our side of the fight.'

'Yes, I noticed it didn't take long to brand me a terrorist, but what options did I have? I could have let it go and accepted the fact that my wife and son are dead and that Stuart Boyle had been punished, but that would mean living a lie, because he hasn't been punished. Did you know that he has been arrested three times since my son's death, each time for driving a stolen vehicle?'

'No, I didn't know that. I haven't seen his file yet,' Harvey admitted.

'Does it sound like he has learnt his lesson? I don't think so. He can't claim to have "accidentally" stolen three more cars, because that's something you choose to do.'

'I agree that he deserves a more severe punishment, but that is not for us to decide, Tom. If everyone took the law into their own hands there would be anarchy—you know that. We have to let the courts decide; that's what they are there for. If you feel badly enough, start a legitimate campaign to get the law changed. It has worked for others in the past, and with your record in the services, people would listen.'

'People are listening now, Andrew, and I don't have to spend years fighting an uphill battle while every day reliving the pain of my family's passing.'

There was silence for a moment, and Harvey sensed Gray was once again thinking of his family. He waited for him to continue rather than interrupting his private moment.

'I also considered grabbing him off the street, you know,' Gray continued after almost a minute, 'taking him somewhere nice and quiet and killing him ever so slowly. Trust me, I thought of that many, many times, but his death would have got a brief mention on the news websites, and nothing would have changed. There would be plenty more Stuart Boyles to replace him.'

'I still don't think this is the way, Tom.'

'Andrew, I appreciate that you have a job to do, and that job is to stop me, but I won't be talked out of this. I accepted your call because I wanted to let you know that trying to mount a rescue would be a bad idea. Apart from the fact that you won't get the location of the device, you will be risking the lives of anyone you send. I know that you will be able to pinpoint my location from the cell phone I am using, and it's only a matter of time before you turn up mobhanded, but I warn you that I have had a few weeks to prepare my defences.

'I have early warning systems set up around the perimeter, including motion sensors and infrared cameras, so I will know if anyone gets too close. The area around the facility is mined, with only one way in or out of the building. If you send in people to clear the mines, I can pick them off. The roof is covered in razor wire, motion sensors and a few other surprises, making an aerial assault tricky. Even if someone did manage to get in, they have to take me alive, and I will have plenty of warning, which means plenty of time to kill these five and take my own life. This will be done live on the Internet, and I will let people know the reason why. The government will then have to explain why they risked the lives of five criminals at the expense of thousands.'

'Okay, Tom, I understand your position.'

'Good. I'll be in touch.'

The phone went dead and Harvey returned it to his pocket on his way over to Farsi's desk.

'We have the location. It's an old factory, Sussex Renaissance Potteries, according to the coordinates GCHQ gave me. SO15 are on their way over there as we speak.'

'Call them,' Harvey said, 'and tell them to hang back and observe from a distance. He told me he has prepared his defences, and I don't doubt it. After you've spoken to them, get on to the security firm and see what he spent a hundred and eighty grand on.'

He had a feeling it wasn't anything that was going to aid their cause.

Tom Gray turned to his array of monitors and checked that each was functioning properly. All twelve screens returned a full colour image, and he toggled each between visible light and infrared. Once he was satisfied that they were all working as required, he turned his attention to the motion sensor display. All thirty sensors in and around the perimeter were listed, and each had a green tick next to their designation to signify that a test signal was being sent and received every second. Should one sensor not respond to a sent signal, a red cross would appear and an audible warning would alert him.

With the equipment in working order, he figured he had at least an hour before any police turned up at his location, and his warning to Andrew Harvey would prevent them from rushing in. With time to kill, he turned his attention to feeding the prisoners. This was done by wheeling a trolley up to each boy's chest so that he could reach the food by craning his neck. He could have released one of their hands to let them eat properly, but he'd decided that if they had chosen to behave like animals, they could eat like animals, too. The food was basic: tinned potatoes and Spam, neither of which he had bothered to heat through.

He pushed the trolley up to the first of the boys, Simon Arkin, and removed the tape over his mouth.

'Eat,' he ordered.

'Why're you doing this?' Arkin asked, more than a touch of anxiety in his voice. 'What have I ever done to you?'

'Nothing. You did nothing to me. But that's only because I don't live near you. I'm sure that if I lived within five miles of you,

you would have had no hesitation in nicking my car or breaking into my house.' Gray studied him for a moment. 'How many houses did you burgle?'

Arkin averted his eyes as he calculated his answer. 'Twenty-eight,' he eventually said.

'You see, that's the problem, Simon. You tell me it's twenty-eight, but that's how many convictions you have for burglary. That means you either just lied to me, or you got caught every time you burgled a house. And if you got caught every time, it would have sunk in after the first three or four, and you wouldn't have bothered with the other twenty-odd, would you?'

Arkin kept his head bowed, taking it as a rhetorical question.

'So what is it? Were you lying to me about the number of burglaries, or are you really so stupid that you got caught every time and yet kept doing it?'

'About three hundred,' Arkin finally admitted. 'But it wasn't just me.'

'I know. I read your record. So why didn't you give the others up when you got caught? The police knew you weren't acting alone, but they were unable to force you to give up the names of the people who were with you. That's what I am going to change.

'As for you, did you ever spare a thought for your victims? Did you ever stop to think how it might impact them?'

'They were all insured, so they didn't lose anything,' Arkin came back, a little too quickly to make the reply sound spontaneous. It was obvious to Gray that it was a line he spouted to all who questioned his career choice, be they the police or social workers.

'Well, let me tell you something about insurance companies, Simon. They don't get a call saying "I've been burgled" and run round to replace everything. They do all they can to put the blame on the homeowner, trying to prove that they were at fault for making it easy for the burglar. For example, if you opened a front door, grabbed the keys of a brand new Mercedes and drove it away, the insurance company will say the blame lies with the homeowner for not securing the keys properly. They lose their forty grand motor and don't get a penny back.'

Gray placed a cup of water next to Arkin's plate and popped a straw in so that he could drink from it. 'You know, it's ironic that you never spared a thought for your victims, because now there are three hundred families out there about to vote on whether you live or die. Not just them, but their friends and families, too. That's thousands of people all voting, and I don't think many will be asking for you to be set free to heap more misery on them. Oh, and don't forget everyone else in the country who has been burgled in their lifetime. I don't think you can count on their votes, either.'

Gray left Arkin to his banquet, satisfied with the look of impending doom on his face. He wheeled a trolley into the next cell and again removed the tape from the young man's mouth.

'Why are you doing this to me?' his prisoner asked. Faced with the prospect of repeating his little speech, Gray said, 'Shut up, dickhead, and eat your dinner.'

Once the prisoners had been fed and watered, he took a stroll around the outside of the building. The factory had once produced earthenware and stood in its own grounds. He had chosen it because it sat well back from the main road, affording him plenty of notice should anyone approach. The sole remaining building was two stories high and in pretty good repair. Most of the windows had been smashed, and Gray had broken the others before boarding them up using two-inch-thick planks.

The four sides of the building had been cleared away, and there were thirty yards of ground which an attacking force would have to cover. Apart from the chance of being picked off by Gray, they would have to negotiate waist-high razor wire and numerous motion sensors, not to mention the anti-personnel mines. Beyond the open ground there were swathes of knee-high grass and the remnants of the other factory buildings that once stood proud but were now reduced to rubble. If anyone wanted to mount an attack, there was little in the way of protection within a hundred and fifty yards of the building.

After checking the perimeter, he returned to the building and began removing the feeding trolleys from the cells, which had once been walk-in kilns. At the first cell, Arkin asked to go to the toilet.

'You're sitting on a commode, so just go when you need to. It will get a bit uncomfortable after a while, but this will all be over in five days ... if not sooner.' He placed a new strip of tape over Arkin's mouth as he began to protest, and went to tend to the prisoner in the next cell.

Chapter Six

Diane Lane walked over to Harvey's desk and handed him a sheaf of papers. 'These are his known acquaintances, ordered by last date of contact. The most recent was two days ago, when he contacted the first six names on the list.'

Harvey took the list, skipped to the last page and noted that the last entry was number 204. 'That's a lot to get through. Let's take the top ten on the list and hand the remainder over to the local police,' he told her.

'My thought exactly. I've been in touch with Scotland Yard, and they're disseminating the list to all local forces as we speak.' She handed Harvey a thick file. 'These are police reports regarding the missing boys. When we speak to these people, we need to ascertain their whereabouts at the times the boys disappeared.'

'Good work, Diane. Let's go and have a chat with them. You take these three,' Harvey said, circling three names, 'I'll take these two, and Hamad can have numbers three, five and six. Before we go, get onto GCHQ, ask them to monitor all calls and emails, in and out, for the top ten names on the list.'

As if on cue, Farsi arrived and made a beeline for Harvey's desk. 'I brought the contractor in to speak to Gerald. Much of what he told me went over my head, and I thought it best to let him talk to someone who also spoke geek. From what I did understand, a lot of the stuff he asked for was pretty routine, although

Gray had some specifications for communicating with a website in Jo'burg.'

'Yeah, we already made the South African connection. Gerald's working on it.'

Farsi began to remove his jacket, but Harvey stopped him. 'We've got a couple of his old army buddies to visit.' He jotted down the names and addresses and handed them to Farsi, along with the police reports. 'Make a note of the dates and times and see if you can tie either of them into their disappearance.' As an afterthought he asked, 'What of the security firm?'

'They emailed his order over, along with basic descriptions, but they can't go too deep into capabilities and weaknesses, as they are only distributors. We'll need to go to the manufacturers for those, and I don't think it's going to be easy at this time on a Sunday.'

'Hand it over to Gerald's team. They must have some kind of technical support service, and if they don't get any joy there, they should go direct to the CEO. We need to know what we're up against and what we can do to get round his defences.'

Farsi nodded his understanding, and Harvey stood up and grabbed his jacket. 'Let's go rattle some cages.'

* * *

The constant beeping of the motion sensor panel heralded the arrival of the authorities. Gray looked at the sensor's designation, and it told him the area was covered by camera twelve, so he switched to the bank of monitors and maximised the view for that camera.

There had been several false alarms earlier in the day, caused by local wildlife, but what he saw on the screen was no bunny rabbit: two figures dressed in black were snaking through the grass two hundred and seventy yards from the side of the building, heading towards the cover of a pile of rubble left by the demolition of an old outbuilding. The remaining wall, which stood barely three feet high, offered the best cover available around the main building, and it was for this reason that Gray had deployed a couple of microphones. One was hidden in the rubble to the side of the wall, and the other was embedded in the wall itself. Gray had drilled through the mortar from the side facing the building, using a drill bit measured to the thickness of the wall minus three millimetres, and so it hadn't broken through the other side of the mortar.

In about twenty minutes the two figures would arrive at the wall, and he would see if the microphones functioned as well in the rain as they did in the dry conditions when he had tested them.

Sergeant Dave Williams of the Metropolitan Police's Counter Terrorism Command, better known as SO15, reached the wall moments before Officer Ben Knightly. He used his binoculars to scan the area between his location and the building and didn't like what he saw.

'It's just like they said, this guy knows how to set a perimeter. We've got shorter grass for about seventy yards, then open ground for another forty. I say open, but I can see barbed wire and mounds everywhere. There's no way we get across there in a hurry.' Williams scanned the front of the building. 'We've got three cameras, sweeping in a one-hundred-and-sixty-degree arc ... wait ... Shit. One is static, looking straight at us. He knows we're here.'

'Do we try another approach?' Knightly asked.

'Hang on.' Williams reached for his thermal-imaging camera to see if he could detect any heat sources in the building, but he was met with a wall of white blobs, dancing around like some kind of psychedelic waltz.

'He's got some kind of disruption system heating every wall. I can't see a thing in there.'

'Now what?'

'We report in and wait for instructions.'

Gray watched their approach on the camera and heard every word they said. He couldn't hear the response from their commanders, but at least they appreciated the effort that had gone into his defences. More importantly, the thermal sheets lining the walls worked. If they couldn't see into the room with heat-detecting equipment, they were virtually blind, adding more uncertainty to the chances of a forced entry succeeding.

As a security consultant Gray was up to date on all of the latest gadgets, and this gave him the edge when it came to defeating SO15. He had searched the Internet for the most state-of-the-art devices that could be used against him, and then trawled through freedom of information documents to see what equipment was available to the various police forces.

Once he knew which thermal-imaging camera SO15 would be likely to deploy, defeating it was relatively easy.

The background work had certainly paid off.

He turned his attention to his laptop, and after watching the vote count tick over the million mark, he folded his arms and laid back in the chair, the hypnotic hum of the diesel generator helping him to sleep. If they decided to launch an attack, operational sense dictated that it would most likely come in the middle of the night, and he planned to be wide awake for it.

Harvey peered through the front window of the terrace house but saw no sign of life. He returned to the door and rang the bell again, but after having drawn a blank at the first suspect's home, he knew he was wasting his time here, too.

'He's not in,' a voice said. It belonged to Tristram Barker-Fink's next-door neighbour, a woman in her sixties, who was standing in her doorway, arms folded and a cigarette dangling from her lips.

'Do you know where he went?' Harvey asked.

'You the police?' she asked, the cigarette bobbing with every word.

'No, I'm an old friend of Tris. We were in the army together. I was hoping to catch up with him while I'm in town on business.'

'I think he went on holiday. He left last week with a holdall and hasn't been back since.'

'Did he say where he was going?' Harvey asked, praying that the old cow was as nosey as he hoped.

'No idea—he just left. He doesn't talk much, that one, and only has men round...' She left the statement hanging, letting Harvey come to his own conclusions. He realised that he wasn't going to get much from this homophobe, so he told her he would try next time he was in town and returned to his car. Once inside he called Hamad Farsi. 'Get anything?' he asked him.

'Len Smart wasn't home, but Carl Levine's wife said he went on a job last week. He told her it was a two-week bodyguard assignment for a visiting dignitary, and she has no reason to doubt him as that's how he earns his living.'

'Okay, check that out with Gray's old company; see if Levine is still on their books. If he isn't, get onto all the security firms in the area to see who he's signed up with.' Harvey hung up, then called Diane Lane. 'What news?' he asked.

'No joy. I've been to all three properties, and none of them are there. I got no answer from Paul Bennett, and Jeff Campbell's wife said he was on an assignment. Same with Colin Avery.'

'Both two-week assignments for visiting dignitaries, by any chance?' Harvey asked.

'Those exact words,' Lane confirmed.

'Then these are our guys. One or two being away is possible, but all eight? I don't think so. Pass their names to Special Branch and tell them it's a priority. We need to find these guys, and quick.'

Tom Gray woke after forty minutes and checked his monitors. The two men were still lying behind the wall, but their command structure had moved in, setting up three vehicles in the lane which ran parallel to the building, two hundred yards from the rear wall. Gray guessed they had closed the lane to prevent the press and members of the public from getting too close. They had also set up a perimeter around the area, with men stationed a hundred feet apart and looking out rather than towards the building. Not only did this suit the authorities by keeping nosey civilians and the media at arm's length, it made life easier for him by preventing those same people setting off his motion sensors every two minutes.

He turned his attention to the TV and caught the tail end of the five o'clock news. They were showing a press conference held by Greater Manchester Police, and Simon Arkin's mother was making an impassioned plea for his release.

'I am asking the people of England to vote for my son's freedom. Yes, he may have a criminal record, but he has been to court and he has been punished.'

Gray watched as she struggled to compose herself, before she gave up the fight and burst into tears.

'I just want my boy back.'

The chief inspector reiterated her plea for the population to do the decent thing before they cut back to the studio. Gray picked up his mobile phone and dialled a preset number.

The BBC News anchor had just finished reading the headlines at six o'clock when she paused for a moment and listened to the message in her earpiece.

'I'm told we now have Tom Gray from the Justice For Britain website on the phone. Mr Gray, thank you for speaking to us today.'

'Hello, Charlene.'

'Mr Gray, I imagine the first question the viewers would be asking is "Why exactly are you doing this?"'

'You know, a few people have asked me that today. My answer is, to ensure that when criminals are caught, they are punished.'

'But as we have just heard from Mrs Arkin, her son was caught, and he has been punished. We also have a justice system that ensures people are punished appropriately. Why do you think we need to change the current system?'

'I think it needs to change because the word "punishment" is being used without anyone properly interpreting the definition. Punishment means any change in a human's surroundings that occurs after a given behaviour or response which reduces the likelihood of that behaviour occurring again in the future. This means that to punish someone is to make them think twice about doing it again. As you can see from the list of convictions on the website, none of the criminals I am holding have had any kind of sentence that made them think twice.

'Let's take Stuart Boyle, for instance. After killing my son, he spent less than eight months in custody. If that was meant to teach him a lesson, it failed badly, because he has been convicted of car theft three times since his release.'

'But surely killing him is a bit extreme. We don't even have the death penalty for murder.'

'Well, that is what this week is all about. Is it too extreme, or has he shown that his only purpose in life is to cause misery to others? If his only contribution to our society is going to be stealing other people's hard-earned possessions, should we have to put up with that? Anyway, I am not the one to decide if he lives or dies; it is the choice of the people. If the people think he should be set free, he will be set free. If they think he should die, he will die.'

'Mr Gray, it sounds like you are trying to deflect the blame away from yourself and on to the people of this country, but the fact remains that it will be you that pulls the trigger, as it were.'

'I am not trying to shift the blame, Charlene. If I kill any of these boys, then I will be guilty of murder, plain and simple.'

'What do you say to suggestions that anyone who votes for the boys to die is an accessory to that murder?'

'I heard the suggestion that voting for a boy to die makes you an accessory to murder, and I think it is ludicrous, something thought up by the government to dissuade people from voting. If twenty million people vote for Simon Arkin to die, what are the government going to do to them? Imprison them all? Fine them all? Every single case would have to go to court, and that would cripple the judicial system that everyone suddenly seems to cherish.'

'What is your suggestion for dealing with repeat offenders, Mr Gray? Do you think they should all be killed?'

'Actually, Charlene, that's what I called about. The guests you have had on this show seem to think that my only objective is to kill these five people. If that was the case, they would all be dead by now. What I really want is to get the people of Britain and, more importantly, the government, thinking about introducing punishments that will eradicate recidivism.

'If your viewers go to the website, they will find a new link that says "Justice Bill" at the top of the page. If they click this link, they will see my recommendations and will be able to vote as to whether they support it or are against it.'

The anchor paused a moment as voices passed on the next question. 'What recommendations are you making, Mr Gray?'

'First of all, no more hiding behind the Human Rights Act. When a crime is committed, someone's human rights have been violated. The person who commits that crime should have his human rights revoked.

'Secondly, the reintroduction of corporal punishment for second offences. First offences can be dealt with as they currently are, but if someone re-offends, they will be birched.

'Next, repeat offenders will be fined the amount in police man-hours it cost to bring them to justice. This will mean we can afford more police on the streets.

'For third offences, conscription. Criminals will be drafted into a special regiment in the army and paid minimum wage, with food and board deducted at source. From their remaining salary they will be given 30 percent, and the rest will go towards paying for the police time it took to bring them to justice. On top of that, they will pay compensation to their victims. Finally, they will pay three thousand pounds towards the cost of forming the new regiment. Once these debts have been paid off, they will spend a further five years in the army on normal salary.'

While Gray was reciting his list, the anchor was receiving yet more instructions from her producer. 'Mr Gray, what if a second offender cannot pay the amount you are suggesting?'

'Then they are conscripted.'

'And what if they don't cooperate once they are conscripted? What if they refuse to follow the army regimen?'

'Then they are sent to prison for as long as it would have taken to pay off their financial debt, plus ten years. And when I say "prison", I mean a real prison, not the cosy hotels we currently have. There are more details of my idea of prisons on the website.'

'So what about ... '

'Sorry, Charlene, but I have said my piece for today. I will call again tomorrow after the government have given their assessment on my suggestions.'

Gray hung up, satisfied that he had handled himself well. He had faced enemy fire, but that was nothing compared to a phone call with a few million eavesdroppers.

With the time approaching six thirty in the evening, he checked the number of votes cast: there were almost four million, and it wasn't looking good for Simon Arkin.

Chapter Seven

John Hammond walked past Harvey's desk and gestured for him to follow. They headed for Gerald Small's office, where they found him deep in conversation with the contractor.

'Gerald, what's the latest?' Hammond asked.

'Alan here has been through the site with me and confirms that there are no booby traps. However, the results aren't counted here. When Gray clicks a button, the website speaks to the South African web service, and it sends back the two counts.'

'That's right,' the contractor said, 'Gray told me that he had commissioned other software in Jo'burg, and all I had to do was send the IP addresses to his email address when the site first kicked off, to get the votes from this web service.'

'Would it be possible to alter this code to change the results in our favour?' Hammond asked Small.

'Sure, that would only take one line of code. However, he gave us easy access to this code, knowing that we would be able to alter it. My guess is that he has other software, and this website is just to test us, to see if we interfere with it. I doubt that he is relying on the results this website will display.'

Hammond thanked the contractor for his time and asked one of the techies to show him out, then asked Small about the other software.

'That,' Small said, 'remains a mystery. We got in touch with the company he paid the fifty grand to, but they were simply instructed to source a developer and pass the details on to Gray. They did just that and got five grand for their trouble. We tried contacting the guy they commissioned, but there was no reply, so we tried the airlines and found out he boarded a plane for Manila two days ago, due to return in three weeks time. The ticket was purchased last week.'

'Which means we have no idea what traps he has in place for us?' Harvey guessed.

'Exactly,' Small confirmed. 'We're blind. Once the emails get to his inbox, we have no idea what he is doing with them.'

'Then we go with the first choice,' Hammond said. 'Intercept the emails before he gets them, and change the odds in our favour. Do it now, we have less than an hour before voting closes.'

Small had everything prepared, and with a few keystrokes he announced it done. 'Every second and third email with "Die" in the body will now be changed to "Live",' he announced.

'Why second *and* third?' Harvey asked.

'If we only do the second,' Small explained, 'the first and second votes will simply cancel each other out and we will be relying on people to send in freedom votes. This way, for every three death votes, we turn them into one net freedom vote. If he is watching the figures in real time, he will still see death votes coming in, but there will be a surge in freedom votes. He will hopefully put it down to the mother's plea.'

'Okay,' Hammond said, 'while we're waiting for the results, check with the Met and find out how they're doing with the search for the device.'

Harvey nodded, and on his way to his desk he stopped off at Farsi's station. 'Anything in the boys' reports?' he asked.

'There were two cases where the kid who was abducted was with his mates. I think we should get them in and show them some mug shots of our suspects.'

'Good idea. Go for it.' Harvey saw Hammond heading for his office and stopped him to explain their plan.

'That could be very useful,' Hammond agreed. 'Gray has no family, so if we can implicate his old army buddies, we might have some leverage. He must have some allegiance to them, and they to him, so if we can pin the abductions on them, we might be able to convince him to end this.'

Harvey saw what Hammond was thinking. 'We can tell Gray they will get immunity from prosecution if he gives himself up; otherwise, we charge them with kidnapping, ABH, accessory to murder and various offences under the Terrorism Act, and send them to jail for life.'

'My point exactly.'

Harvey turned to Farsi. 'Get on to the company he sold, and tell them to send over photos of everyone on their books, past and present, and then arrange for them to be distributed to the police forces handling these cases.'

Harvey was going through the incoming reports from the dozens of police forces around the country. So far they had identified, among them, over a thousand locations that would normally have thousands of visitors at midday on Friday. Many had already been searched and discarded, but at the current rate, there would still be over three hundred to search when the deadline arrived. Shopping centres were being asked to utilise all available staff in searching their own facilities, as were other venues such as exhibition centres and museums. Despite their efforts, though, police were still required to visit each site and give it the once-over before it was given the all-clear.

Even if all possible venues were cleared before the deadline, there was always the possibility that the device might be mobile and delivered much nearer the time, negating their efforts. The only way to be certain was to get Gray to reveal the location, but he had stopped answering his phone and certainly wasn't going to give that information up readily. If they could just get a break somewhere along the line, they might stand a chance of stopping this, but as things stood, Gray still held all the best cards.

Harvey glanced at his watch and saw that the voting would close in ten minutes: time to visit Gerald and see how things were progressing.

At Small's desk he found him staring at the screen. 'How's it going?' Harvey asked.

'The numbers are working in our favour. Around 75 percent of them wanted Simon dead, but that has swung our way now. With that same 75 percent wanting him to be set free.'

'How does that affect the overall result?'

'That we don't know. The exchange server is simply a relay, forwarding the emails onto another server, so we don't have a history to look at.'

'So we just cross our fingers and hope?'

'Yep, that's all we can do now. Thing is, though, even if we didn't manage to do it in time to save Simon, it should save the lives of the others.'

'If he falls for it.'

Harvey went to Hammond's office to see what he made of Gray's list of proposed law changes. 'Is there anything sensible in his justice bill?'

'On the face of it,' Hammond said, 'the public will probably lap this up, but some of it just isn't possible—his idea of a real jail, for starters.'

'What is he suggesting?'

Hammond looked through the printout to find the details. 'Each prisoner will have their own cell, and they will stay in there for twenty-three hours a day. Meals will be served in their cells. There will be one hour of exercise per day, each person in a separate compound, and no contact between prisoners whatsoever. Each prisoner will be given work to do in their cell, and if they meet their daily target, they get eight hours pay at minimum wage, minus food and board, plus two hours of television. If they don't meet their daily target, they get another day added to their sentence and no pay. Once they have paid off the cost of their prosecution they have the option of moving into the prison population to serve their sentence, or remaining on their work schedule and taking courses to give them a chance on the outside. If they do this, they get extra privileges, such as more TV and more exercise time, and each extra day of work takes two days off their sentence.'

'Sounds like he's got it all worked out. Does he say what kind of work they would be doing?'

'To start off with, they could assemble pens and other items that require little quality control. The courses will be in areas such as website design, computer maintenance and office skills. Registered charities will be able to commission websites, get their PCs fixed and so on.'

'I guess he wants to revoke their human rights so that they can be forced to work.'

'It certainly looks like it,' Hammond agreed. 'That, and the reintroduction of the birch.'

'Reintroduction? I thought the birch was only used on the Isle of Man,' Harvey said.

'More recently, yes, but my father told me about the time he was given six strokes on the bare arse when he was a teenager. He was one of the last to get the birch, and the judge told him that if he had been a little older, he would probably have been given the cat o' nine tails. My father said it was a very effective form of punishment, and looking back, he said it was a shame they abolished judicial corporal punishment in 1948.'

'Perhaps Gray has a point. When I was at school, they had the cane and the slipper, and it made you think twice.'

'Yes, Gray mentions that, too. He claims that back in the eighties there was none of the antisocial behaviour that plagues our country today, and he thinks it's because schools knew how to discipline kids. These days, teachers can't even shout at their pupils without being sued by the parents.'

'Is he demanding that these changes are implemented before Thursday?' Harvey asked.

'No. Again, he wants the people to decide. He wants the government to promise to hold a referendum one year from now, but only if the majority of the votes through his website are for his proposals. He says that holding a referendum gives both opponents and supporters of the changes the chance to put their arguments forward.'

'So they should promise him a referendum, and when it's all over they can retract.'

'Oh, our Mr Gray thought of that, don't you worry. He said the government can refuse to hold a referendum if they wish, but in doing so they admit that they are happy to let repeat offenders back on the street time and time again. With the whole country glued to this story, and with millions of them having been victims of crime in recent years, I don't think the current administration will be very popular at the upcoming election. If they promise to hold the referendum and retract later, they will be seen to lie to the people.'

'It looks like Gray has it all worked out,' Harvey said. 'Mind you, he has had months to prepare this, and we only have days to stop him.'

'That's usually the case, Andrew, but criminals never think of everything. We just have to find the one flaw in his plan.' Hammond rose and put on his jacket. 'I'm going to grab some dinner before the main show. I'll be back before eight thirty.'

Hammond left the building and pulled his collar up to combat the evening chill, hoping that his assertion was correct and that there was indeed a flaw in Gray's plan.

In his thirty-seven years in the service, he had been through many scrapes and overcome many adversaries, but the vast majority of the time they had been aware of the threat early on and had the time and resources to deal with it. Tom Gray had turned all that on its head, putting them on the back foot from the start and leaving them very little room for manoeuvre.

If there wasn't a flaw in Gray's plan, if this was a no-win situation, then people were going to die, and there was nothing he could do about it.

Chapter Eight

'Hi.

'Well, it's time to find out what will happen to Simon Arkin. I'm not going to hype this up because this isn't something I'm relishing. I am only doing this because I personally think the government have failed us when it comes to punishing criminals, repeat offenders in particular.

'The results will appear on your page any moment now. There is no need to refresh your browser, it will do it automatically.' Gray stared off to the left of the camera, his face illuminated by the reflection of the web page he was studying. He looked over to the right of the camera, then back to the web page. After a few moments of contemplation, he addressed his audience once more.

'You will see that the majority of the votes on your screen want me to free Simon Arkin. The results are: Live, four million, eight hundred and six thousand, two hundred and five; Die, three million, six hundred and fifty one thousand, eight hundred and eighty four.'

Gray stood and positioned the camera towards Simon's cell. He entered, moved to his right and put his hand out towards the wall. Moments later the single bare bulb suspended over the struggling prisoner flickered into life.

Harvey, Hammond and Small, along with millions of others, watched as Tom Gray stood in front of Simon Arkin, staring at the figure in the chair. Harvey was about to refresh the page, thinking the feed had frozen, when Gray suddenly drew his weapon, an automatic pistol, and fired a single shot. The execution was obscured by Gray's frame, but as he approached Arkin and checked the pulse on his neck, Harvey saw a red patch growing around the slumped figure's heart.

'Shit,' Harvey muttered.

On the screen, Gray turned off the light and closed the cell door before returning to speak to the camera. 'I have several computers based around the country, each one sending emails at the rate of one per minute, using a different email address each time. These emails are stored in a database which matches the outgoing email database, and checks that each has arrived and that they haven't been tampered with. All of the emails had "Die" in the body, but they were never counted in the final vote. However, it seems that a number of them have been changed to "Live" along the way.

'We will never know the actual results, because the government have interfered with the voting. I asked them not to interfere. In fact, I think I made it pretty clear that they shouldn't interfere, but they ignored my warnings. That is why Simon Arkin won't be going home today.'

Gray spent a moment on his laptop, then addressed the camera again.

'Okay, the database has been reset, and voting for the next candidate—Adrian Harper—starts now. Adrian is nineteen, from Gravesend, Kent, and his crimes include aggravated burglary, assault, and numerous counts of theft of a motor vehicle. It's time to get emailing. Don't forget to vote on my proposed law changes, too. Just click the "Justice Bill" link at the top of the screen for further instructions.'

Gray sat back in his chair. 'I will be back at the same time tomorrow, when hopefully the results will reflect the views of the people of Britain, not the views of the government.'

'Shots fired! Shots fired!'

'Understood. Wait one, repeat, wait one.' The commander at the scene, Superintendent Evan Davies, had been watching the video feed and heard the report from Sergeant Williams just as the scene unfolded on his laptop. His orders were to observe and report only until he received direct instructions from HQ, regardless of what happened. Headquarters would have seen the shooting, and moments later he got the call he was expecting. 'Stand down. I say again, stand down.'

'We have shots fired,' Davies said, more for protocol than to enlighten his superiors.

'Confirm shots fired, looks like one hostage down. We have no authority to engage at this time, so continue to observe and report only.'

'Roger that, observe and report only. Out.'

Davies glanced again at the map of the target building and the surrounding area. It was covered with markings showing Gray's defences, and truth be told he was glad their remit was limited to observing and reporting. Davies was ex-army himself, and he knew that a half-decent soldier could prepare formidable defences overnight: Gray had been preparing his for months, and what he saw didn't exactly inspire confidence in a successful outcome.

He had passed these observations on to his superiors, and they had acknowledged his assessment, along with his recommendation that this was more suited to the guys at Hereford. He didn't consider this suggestion cowardly, just the optimum way to get things done with the minimum loss of life. His unit had handled many armed sieges with great success, but they had usually been dealing with a single person trapped with nowhere to go, one person who suddenly found himself in a situation he'd never contemplated.

This was a completely different ball game.

⌒

The call from the home secretary came three minutes after the shooting, and Hammond took it in his office.

'Tell me I didn't just see a British man execute another British man, on British soil, live on the Internet,' Wells said without preamble. 'The PM is livid.'

'Mr Home Secretary, I did explain that the plan to manipulate the votes wasn't guaranteed to succeed, but it was the best—no—it was the *only* option we had at the time.'

'And it got a man killed!' Wells shouted down the phone.

Hammond did his best to hold his own temper. 'With respect, Mr Home Secretary, even if we hadn't changed the votes, the result would have been the same. The country voted for that young man to die, and I think *that* should concern the PM more, as it shows how out of touch he is with the electorate. At least now the PM can deflect attention from that fact and spend the next twenty-four hours convincing the population not to sentence the next man to death.'

There was silence for a while as the minister considered the suggestion. 'I shall pass that on to the PM, but needless to say, he will not want a repeat of tonight's debacle.'

The phone went dead, and Hammond stared at the handset for a moment before cradling it gently. They now had no way of manipulating the votes, so he had to focus on the two main priorities. He called Harvey into his office and wasted no time when the group leader arrived.

'Double the efforts on finding that device, and find us something to pin on Gray's associates.'

Chapter Nine

Monday, 18 April 2011

Tom Gray woke just before five in the morning. No one had made a move on the building, and he had managed to grab some sleep just after three o'clock, although the night was far from quiet. Two of his guests had made plenty of noise at around midnight, but after ignoring their muffled calls for a while, he had eventually shut them up for the night with a few well-aimed blows. Stuart Boyle had also played up for a while, but Gray hadn't even entered his cell: he didn't trust himself to show any restraint, and now wasn't the time to deal with him. Mr Boyle's day would come, but today wasn't that day.

After checking that the boys were still with him and secure, he scanned his monitors: no sign of any movement except for up at their control vehicle, where a couple of people were standing around drinking hot drinks and looking bored. *Not long to go, guys,* he thought. This was well beyond their pay grade, and it wouldn't be long before the Regiment was called in to take over. It was unlikely that his former colleagues would ever launch an attack, given the consequences and the defences he had put in place, but they needed to be ready just in case the security services discovered his device. Although Gray knew they would never find it, they would nevertheless be pursuing that line of investigation rigorously.

He made himself some breakfast and watched the figures on his laptop tick over as he ate. Surprisingly, the 'Live' votes were slightly in the lead, so he checked that his countermeasures were still in place and operational. Everything seemed fine, so he ran a code comparison tool which compared the files on the South African web server with the ones on his laptop: they were exactly the same, which meant the code hadn't been interfered with. Next he ran the duplicate email tool and that appeared to be working, too. If anyone tried to send more than one email from the same email address, it would only accept the first as a valid vote: the rest would be recorded on a separate system but not included in the final vote. The same applied to IP addresses, which prevented people from using more than one email account on the same computer. Basically, it was one vote per household. His software had identified over six hundred thousand duplicate emails, which was not unexpected, given the passion some people seemed to have for what was happening.

Gray switched on the news channel and saw a representative from the leading human rights group, Liberty, denouncing his suggestions.

'... is a clear breach of Article Three of the Human Rights Act. How can giving a young person the birch not be considered torture? Article Three defines any treatment which causes intense physical or mental suffering to be inhuman, and inhuman acts are defined as torture. I defy anyone to tell me that the birch does not cause intense physical suffering, not to mention the mental suffering that will inevitably go with it.'

'So how would you suggest we deal with recidivists, Ms. Barker?' the newscaster asked. 'As Tom Gray has pointed out, some people have criminal records as long as their arms, and the current system doesn't seem to be helping them at all.'

'It sounds like you are in favour of his reforms,' the Liberty representative said, much to Gray's amusement.

'Not at all, I'm just trying to engage in an objective debate. You say that corporal punishment is not the answer, so what alternative suggestions does Liberty have?'

Rebecca Barker was clearly annoyed at being put on the spot and did little to hide her displeasure. 'We advocate re-education and community punishments, giving something back to the areas they have affected. Beating criminals has no place in civilised society.'

Gray spotted the own goal and watched the newscaster swoop in for the kill. 'Is Liberty saying that Singapore, The United Arab Emirates and Saudi Arabia are uncivilised countries?'

'No, of course not,' Barker blushed, 'but there are thirty other countries that have judicial corporal punishment, and some of these are far from civilised nations.'

'Such as ... ?'

'Such as Zimbabwe.'

The newscaster nodded, conceding that Barker had made a good choice, but still pressed. 'And of course, in Saudi Arabia, persistent thieves have their hands chopped off. This certainly makes it difficult for them to commit the same crime again, yet Tom Gray is not asking the government to go that far.'

'Yes, it might prevent a criminal from committing the same offence again, but at what cost? Given one more chance, that criminal might have changed his ways and become an upstanding member of society, but by then he has been robbed of that chance.'

'But surely the question is, how many chances does a person need? Is four enough? Or seven? Or should we go on giving them chance after chance indefinitely? I think Tom Gray's point is that there has to come a time when we say "enough", and the criminal has to take full responsibility for his actions.'

Rebecca Barker was becoming flustered at not winning the argument, so she decided to draw the interview to a close. 'We seem to be going round in circles here. Suffice it to say, Liberty's stance is that we strongly condemn any suggestions of reintroducing judicial corporal punishment in the UK.'

The newscaster thanked her and introduced the sports reporter, who began with yet another high-profile football manager losing his job after a run of poor results. Gray had little interest in football, so he scanned his monitors and, once satisfied that no attack was imminent, he prepared a dry breakfast for his guests.

Once they were fed, he sat down at the monitors again and scanned the perimeter. Movement on one of the screens caught his eye: a figure emerged from the control vehicle and passed something to one of the men standing around. The man put his cup down on the step of the vehicle and started walking towards the building. Gray kept the camera on him as he closed the distance, and seventy metres from the building the man stopped and held up a large piece of cardboard. On it were written the words 'Harvey calling'. Gray used the control stick for the camera to move it up and down three times, effectively letting the camera nod his understanding. The figure gave the camera a thumbs-up and Gray watched him retreat before switching his mobile phone back on. It rang within seconds.

'Hello, Andrew,' Gray said.

'Hello, Tom. What you did last night wasn't a very clever move. My bosses are now under enormous pressure to resolve this problem.'

'I think it was. I think it showed people that I mean business, and it will remind your bosses what will happen if anyone tries to interfere again. Last night was just a warning, Andrew. The next time I will kill everyone in the building, including myself. That leaves you with the task of finding my device before midday on Friday, and I very much doubt you will.'

'That brings me on to my next question, Tom,' Harvey said. 'How do we know you actually have a device? I believe you, but my bosses and their bosses want proof. If I can't give it to them, they may start to think there isn't a device at all, and that means you lose all of your bargaining power.'

In the early days of planning this mission, Gray had expected something along these lines, which was why he had forged close ties with the senior management at a research and development company, a company doing hush-hush work for the Ministry of Defence and specialising in the manufacturing of chemical 'deterrents'. Having gained their confidence, he had wangled a tour of the facility on the pretence of providing an independent security assessment.

'What you're telling me is that only twenty-four hours into your search, you haven't found a thing, and now you want me to hand it to you on a plate, is that right?'

'No, just some solid proof that a device exists.'

Gray thought for a moment before answering. 'I expect you've been looking for a huge device, haven't you? You're thinking, "He's going to kill thousands of people, so it must be a really big bomb", aren't you? Well, you're thinking too big. Think smaller. Think airborne.'

'Thanks for that, I appreciate the information, but my superiors will still want proof.'

'Fair enough. Have you heard of a company called Norden Industries?'

'Yes.'

'If you contact them they will confirm that I have made three visits to the facility.'

'Which proves nothing, I'm afraid. I know what they make there, and their stock will be audited on an almost daily basis. If anything was missing, they would know about it by now.'

'Yes, I saw their audit process, and it is quite thorough in one respect. Their full canisters are checked daily, but it is a visual inspection only, and they don't audit the empty canisters. You take an empty canister, fill it with water, and on a subsequent visit you swap it with a full canister.'

Harvey considered the plausibility for a moment, then said, 'Okay, I'll let my superiors know.' He hung up and went straight to Hammond's office, walking in without knocking.

'John, I just spoke to Gray. I managed to get some info about his device, but it needs checking out.' He shared the information he had gained and waited for Hammond's opinion, which was not long in coming.

'Go down there and see for yourself. Get them to go through the audit process and see if Gray's claim holds water. Let me know as soon as you find out so that I can tell the police to adapt their search.'

'Will do. Would you mind calling ahead to explain my visit? It should save time when I get there.'

Hammond nodded and Harvey left, grabbing his coat on his way out of the office. After picking up his car from the underground car park, he drove north to join the A40 and followed it west until it became the M40. The journey to the facility in the Oxfordshire countryside took just over an hour, and after showing his ID, he was quickly waved through the gate. The director of the facility was waiting for him in the reception area.

'Simon Crawford,' he said, extending his hand. Harvey shook it and introduced himself before wasting no time in explaining the reason for his visit.

'I need to witness your audit process for myself to determine if there is a weakness that might have been exploited recently. Do you have video surveillance of the storage area?'

'Yes, we digitally record it,' Crawford said as he led Harvey to the storage facility.

'How long do you keep the recordings for?'

'Thirty days, in accordance with government regulations.'

'When did Tom Gray visit the facility?' Harvey asked.

'He has been here three times: February 8th, February 26th and March 7th.'

'So his last visit was more than thirty days ago. Very convenient.'

Crawford led him to the storage wing, and after passing through two layers of security, Harvey was led through a door into an enormous warehouse. Looking left and right, he could see over a hundred feet in each direction, and as he followed Crawford he counted off twelve rows of refrigeration units.

'How many fridges are here?' Harvey asked.

'Five hundred and fifty.' Crawford said.

'So how many canisters in total?'

'Yesterday's closing count was forty-three thousand, six hundred and ten. There will have been a handful more added today.'

Harvey walked to a fridge at random and asked Crawford to demonstrate a typical audit. Crawford activated his tablet PC and brought up the stock page relating to the fridge Harvey had chosen. 'There should be eighty-six capsules in here,' he said, and did a swift count to confirm the amount. He then pulled out the first canister. Like all the others, it was a six-inch-long cylindrical container with a valve system at the top, rather like a very small scuba tank, Harvey thought. It was contained within a Perspex box, and Harvey could see a label on the cylinder. Crawford pulled a penlike device from his tablet and scanned the barcode, satisfied to see a match on the screen.

'What do you use to generate that barcode?' Harvey asked.

Crawford seemed to squirm at that question, and Harvey pressed him on it. 'That seems to have hit a nerve,' he said.

'Mr Gray asked me the same question, and I told him that it was standard third-party software. He suggested that these labels could easily be replicated and recommended a company which offered a barcode generator with a unique key, so replication would be impossible.'

'And did you take his advice on board?' Harvey asked.

'I passed it along to my bosses, along with his other sugges-tions, and they took it under advisement,' Crawford admitted sheepishly.

'So knowing that the barcode was created using standard third-party software, Gray could easily have made his own, is that correct?'

'I suppose so,' Crawford admitted, 'but what good would that do him?'

'Off the top of my head, he creates a label identical to one in these fridges. During his first or second visit he steals an empty canister and photographs a label from one of these canisters. He takes the empty canister home, fills it with water, creates the appropriate label and on a subsequent visit he switches canisters, meaning one of these canisters now contains water and Tom Gray is threatening the country with something very nasty. How does that sound?'

Crawford ran through the scenario and matched it with the current security procedures. Harvey watched as the colour drained from his face. 'But how would he make the swap?' Crawford asked. 'He was accompanied by a member of staff at all times.'

'A simple diversion would be my guess. Unfortunately, you don't have video surveillance for any of his visits, so we can't say one way or the other that he actually managed to make a swap. With that said, I want you to take a sample from each of these canisters to make sure they contain what they should contain.'

'But that's over thirty-four thousand canisters! It will take weeks to test them all because each canister will have to be checked manually to determine the contents.'

'Can't you narrow it down to agents that will kill thousands if dispersed at altitude?'

'Mr Harvey, we don't make deodorant or perfume here. *Everything* in this room has that capability.'

'Then I suggest you get started,' Harvey told him. 'I don't care if you have to hire extra staff and work three shifts a day, I want every canister checked. If you have any issues with this, please let me know, and my boss will only be too happy to have a word with the home secretary and the defence secretary. Your career will be over before you can say, "How the fuck did I end up on the dole"?'

He walked towards the exit and had to wait for Crawford to gather himself before he joined him and took him to the facility entrance. Once outside, Harvey thought he might have been too harsh with the director of the facility. With this being a government-run facility, his hands were probably tied when it came to the budget, and he probably had request after request denied by his bosses, who would then blame him for any shortcomings. This particular incident wasn't going to sit nicely with them.

Still, they were facing a crisis, and there wasn't time to play Mr Nice Guy, so he dismissed the thought and called Hammond to pass on the news. 'The threat is credible,' he told his boss.

'What did he take?' Hammond asked.

'We don't know if he took anything yet. However, if he managed to sneak out with a single canister, the results aren't going to be pretty.' He described the canisters so that Hammond could pass the information on to the police, and then got into his car for the drive back to Thames House. A whole day had been wasted looking in the wrong places, which left just four days to search the whole country for a device the size of a can of hairspray. Needle in a haystack just didn't come close.

Chapter Ten

Evan Davies climbed out of the command vehicle and went to meet the occupants of the black Land Rover which had just pulled up. He was surprised to see just two figures, the driver and passenger, emerge from the vehicle. The passenger approached and offered Davies his hand. 'Major Sean Blythe, and this is Sergeant Todd Dennis. We'll be taking over command of this operation.'

Davies introduced himself and led them into his command vehicle.

'Have you been in contact with him?' Blythe asked.

'No,' Davies said. 'We do have a couple of mobile numbers for him, but we just get voicemail every time we try.' He brought out a map of the building and surrounding area. 'These are the defences we have been able to identify so far,' he said, gesturing to the area representing the back of the building. 'He has wall cameras mounted here, here and here, each of them multidirectional. In the clear ground he has a maze of razor wire, with a few land mines thrown in for good measure. We have been unable to penetrate any walls using thermal imaging, as he has some kind of heated insulation, and directional microphones are just getting white noise from the building.

'The same goes for the two sides of the building and most of the front as well. The only exception is a path leading up to the main door. The path itself is one metre wide and concrete all the way to the door. The razor wire stops either side of the path, so you have a clear walk up to the front door. Why he left the path clear, I don't know. From what he said on the website, I don't think he's planning on coming out, and I shouldn't think he'd want to give an assault team a clear run at the building.'

'He most likely did it so that the hostages that are freed don't blow themselves up on their way out,' Dennis suggested, 'but we should also view it as a bottleneck. By offering us this route in, he is concentrating bodies into a small area, which means a couple of well-placed claymores and anyone on the path is spaghetti.'

'So, going in on the ground is going to be tough, which leaves an assault from above or below,' Davies said. 'The roof has razor wire all over it, as well as some packages which we can't make out. They could be explosives, we just don't know. There is a large sewer complex under the building, but if you consider the path a bottleneck, the sewer will be a whole lot worse.'

Dennis studied the map, frowning in concentration. 'It's all academic at the moment, as we can't go in until his bomb is located. However, we need a plan in place for that eventuality. Do you have schematics for the interior?'

'We've requested them, and they're on their way over,' Davies told him.

'Okay, let me know when they arrive.' Dennis folded the map and stuck it inside his leather jacket, excused himself and swapped the command vehicle for his own. He drove off in the direction he had come from, and mentally prepared the briefing for his troops. They were going to like this as much as he did, and he didn't like it one little bit.

———

As the man walked into the mosque, he got a few cursory glances from those making their way out, but nothing more. He sat on a bench and removed his shoes before striding across the prayer floor towards the imam's personal quarters, and at the door he was confronted by two young men who moved to block his way.

'The imam is busy,' the first one told him, holding out a hand to stop the stranger.

'He will see me,' the man said confidently. 'Tell him I bring greetings from Quetta.' He was referring to the capital of the province of Balochistan, forty miles from the border with Afghanistan, and the name struck a chord. The guards shared a glance, and one of them knocked on the imam's door before walking in, closing it behind him. A moment later the door opened again, and the guard reappeared, gesturing for the stranger to enter.

The imam stood and came round his desk as his visitor entered the spartan room. The man before him wore traditional Pakistani attire and had a full, thick beard, much like many members of the mosque, but he was certain the man hadn't been to prayers recently. Yet there was something strikingly familiar about the stranger, like a faint memory from long ago, and deep in his mind's eye he found the answer.

'Ahmed?'

'Brother,' the man said, opening his arms for an embrace which was reciprocated. The imam then instructed the guard to bring tea and close the door on the way out.

'What brings you back, Ahmed?' the imam asked.

'I have instructions from our benevolent masters,' Ahmed said. 'You have no doubt seen the news recently.'

'This man holding his own country to ransom? He is a fool.'

'Why do you say that, brother?'

'Because he will achieve nothing,' the imam said. 'The British government will never give in to his demands.'

'They have so far, have they not?' Ahmed pointed out. 'They do not attack him because he has put fear in their hearts with his so-called device. And now the time has come to exploit and enhance that fear.'

'What do you have in mind?' the imam asked.

'First I need enough true believers to see this plan through.'

'How many do you need?'

'I have a list of men who have been to the training camps and need you to bring them in. We also need as many others as you can find.'

'Give me the names, and I will bring them to you,' the imam told him. 'I can also give you twenty others who are willing to do Allah's bidding.'

'Excellent, but time is against us,' Ahmed said, 'so we must move swiftly. I need these men here by four o'clock tomorrow afternoon. I will reveal the assignment when all are together, and, *Inshallah*, we will strike fear in the hearts of these people.'

'*Inshallah.*'

God willing.

Tom Gray listened to the news as he scanned his monitors. Nothing was happening outside, and even less was happening on the TV. That was the trouble with a rolling news channel, he thought: unless they had a breaking story it was the same thing over and over again. However, his curiosity was aroused when the newscaster announced an imminent interview with the home secretary '... live on air, straight after the weather.'

Gray took the opportunity to check on his guests again, then sat down to see what the bloated politician had to say. Stephen Wells was introduced to the viewers and fielded an easy opening question.

'Mr Home Secretary, what progress has been made in the search for Tom Gray's bomb?'

'Police forces all over the country are working day and night to try and locate the device Mr Gray claims to have. Our security services are also working tirelessly to protect the people of this nation. We are confident that we will see a peaceful resolution to this episode.'

I'm threatening to kill thousands and he calls it an episode, Gray thought. *Talk about playing it down.*

'Do we know what kind of bomb Mr Gray claims to have?' the newscaster asked.

'Not at this moment in time, but we are working hard to ascertain just exactly what kind of threat we are dealing with.'

The newscaster changed tack, possibly hoping to throw the home secretary off his guard.

'What is your response to Mr Gray's proposed law changes?'

The home secretary didn't even break sweat. 'There are fundamental flaws in Mr Gray's proposals which make them unworkable, I'm afraid. For a start, he wants us to conscript criminals into the army and give them guns, while we are working hard to take guns out of the hands of criminals. There is also the cost involved in conscription to consider, and we estimate it would run into the tens of millions.'

'What about reintroducing judicial corporal punishment?'

'This is the twenty-first century, and there is no desire to return to the days of whipping people for stealing a loaf of bread. Although the government respect the rights of other countries to use judicial corporal punishment, Britain has a proud history of reform and re-education.'

'Does this mean the government will refuse to hold a referendum, even if the people of Britain vote for one through Mr Gray's website?'

'We are currently reviewing the judicial system and have been for the last few months. Although we agree with Mr Gray that something needs to be done, we do not always agree on the way to implement any changes we decide to make. Any changes we make will be with a view to reducing crime and setting higher tariffs for the most serious crimes.'

'So does that mean there will be no referendum?' the newscaster pressed. In typical fashion the home secretary simply reworded his previous statement, much to the newscaster's—and Gray's—disappointment. The interview continued for a few more minutes, the newscaster switching between simple and searching questions, and the politician responding with platitudes and spin.

Gray turned to his laptop while the interview was still fresh in his mind and drafted a response. After an hour of editing, he was happy with the copy and picked up his mobile, hitting the speed-dial button for the BBC News studio. After a few rings the phone was answered, and he gave the password he always used to identify himself. Within seconds he was through to the daytime show's producer.

'Hello, Paul,' Gray said. 'I saw the interview with the home secretary and just wanted to give my side of the story. Do you have an email address I can send it to?'

'We can put you on the air, Mr Gray,' the producer said, thinking of the ratings. However, Gray wasn't in the mood for a series of questions. 'No, thank you, Paul. Just give me an email address to send it to, and you can read it out on air.'

'Are you sure? You can make more of an impact with the nation if you ... '

'Paul, give me an email address or I call Sky News instead.'

Paul Gross reeled off his personal email address, and Gray thanked him before hanging up. Within seconds the email was in Gross's inbox, and after a quick scan through he forwarded it to the relevant departments, with instructions.

Gray only had to wait four minutes before his response was ready to be read out, and he followed every word to make sure it hadn't been edited.

'We have just received a statement from Tom Gray in response to the home secretary's earlier interview,' the newscaster said. 'Mr Gray says, "I would like the nation to hear both sides of the story so that they can make their own choice, rather than just accepting the rhetoric the government spew out day after day".'

Gray had wondered if that opening sentence was going a bit too far, but it was too late now.

'"The home secretary said that I want to conscript criminals into the army and give them guns: that is far from the truth. My proposal is that conscripts will be non-combatants throughout their probation period, until they have proven themselves and paid off their debt, and all exercises during that time will use blank ammunition. Control of weapons will be ramped up for conscripts, and live fire will only be used after the probation period is up, and only for those conscripts with an exemplary record. Any conscripts who do not abide by the rules will be sent to prison to work out their sentence, which will leave only reformed members of society within the ranks.

'"The home secretary also states that conscription will cost the nation tens of millions, but as I have already pointed out in my proposal, there were three periods of conscription in the twentieth century: There was the Military Service Act of 1916; the National Service (Armed Forces) Act in 1939; and finally the National Service Act of 1948. If conscription could be introduced in the days of paper records, why not now in the twenty-first century? I should also point out that the cost of setting up the new regiment will be recovered from the conscripts' salaries.

'"Finally, the home secretary said that they prefer reform and re-education to the birch. If reform and re-education work, why are there so many repeat offenders? In 2009, nearly twenty-one thousand offenders who had been convicted or cautioned between twenty-five and fifty times avoided custodial sentences. If they had been birched or conscripted after their second or third convictions, respectively, this would have prevented between four hundred thousand and one million crimes being committed. Then there are the criminals with more than three but less than twenty-five convictions, and not forgetting the criminals with more than fifty convictions or cautions. If the birch and conscription is introduced, it could prevent over four million offences every year. Imagine the saving in police costs, and that is just the ones that were not given a custodial sentence. If my measures were introduced, how do you think the population would react? Would they clamour for these criminals to be set free, or would everyone who has had a crime committed against them in the last twenty years welcome my proposals?"

'Finally, Mr Gray wants us to remind you that you can still vote for or against his proposed changes on his website at www .justiceforbritain.co.uk/justicebill. The results will appear on his website tomorrow at midday.'

Chapter Eleven

Hamad Farsi strode over to Andrew Harvey's desk and waited until the group leader finished his phone call.

'Special Branch picked up Marcus Taylor this morning and showed him some mug shots. He picked out Simon Baines.'

'Marcus Taylor?' Harvey asked, a look of confusion on his face.

'He was with Joseph Olemwu on the night he was abducted,' Farsi reminded him.

'Great news, but it does us no good at all if we can't find these guys. Any news from the security agencies?'

'None. We tried the company Gray sold, and while they are still on the books, they haven't had an assignment for the last two months. We also contacted all security firms on our lists, and none of them have heard of our guys.'

'Have we checked the airports and ferries?' Harvey asked.

'No hits there, either. Unless they got hold of new identities, these guys are still in the country. Gray could have paid for new identities, of course. He has a lot of money unaccounted for, and that's not the kind of thing you buy with a debit card, but some of these guys have families. Do you think it likely that they would abandon them?'

'It's possible, but I doubt it. Let's concentrate our search on guesthouses and bed and breakfasts. They may be together, or they may have dispersed around the country, so let each establishment know we're looking for one or more men matching their descriptions.'

'We can try,' Farsi said, 'but these guys are used to spending weeks in a hole in the Iraqi desert or a sodden field in Bosnia. They could be anywhere in Britain, and if they don't want to be found they could quite easily make themselves disappear. I think the last place they will choose will be a B&B.'

'I know,' Harvey said a little too harshly, 'but we have to start somewhere.'

'Sonny, leave that porn site alone and come and butter this bread. These sausages are nearly ready. Oh, and wash your hands first.'

Simon Baines clipped Tristram Barker-Fink around the back of the head as he passed. 'Cheeky bastard. I was checking the BBC News website.'

'Anything new?' Barker-Fink asked as he turned the sausages.

'Nothing in the last hour,' Sonny said. 'I was looking at some of the readers' comments and there's a lot of support for what Tom's doing. A few nut-jobs want things left as they are, but most of them want a change. A couple of them even called him a hero.'

'I think they have a point. There must be millions of people who have been victims of crime and millions more who fear becoming victims. This bill of his will make a lot of people feel safer, and it only came about because he is willing to risk everything to see it through. That's some sacrifice.'

'If the government agree to implementing it, that is,' Sonny said. 'If they refuse, this has been for nothing.'

'Sonny, if the country votes for this bill, there is no way the government can refuse a referendum.'

'Of course they can; you know what politicians are like. They can spin it every which way and make it sound like they are doing the country a favour. Look at the expenses scandal: they claim to have cleaned everything up, but then they put a new tax avoidance bill through Parliament that closes loopholes for everyone in the country—except MPs, who are still allowed to exploit it. They only care about themselves, and if this bill is going to make life uncomfortable for them, they will drop it like a hot brick.'

'We'll see. The results will be in at noon tomorrow, and twenty-four hours later we'll hear what the PM has to say and this will all be over.'

'And in the meantime we're stuck in this fucking barge,' Sonny said. 'There's no room to move, and we can't even stick our heads out the door. It stinks of farts and sweat, and all we've eaten is egg banjos, sausage sarnies and fry-ups.'

The vessel they were renting was a six-berth narrow boat, although, truth be told, it was designed more for a family with young children than eight burly soldiers, which explained why two of them had such cramped sleeping quarters and another two slept on the floor.

The Norfolk Broads were relatively quiet at this time of year, and with only one person required to pilot the boat, the rest could remain undercover. It had been decided in advance that Carl Levine, with his previous experience of narrow boating, would be the one to show his face, and so he had grown a full-face beard and shaved his head. A pair of sunglasses completed the look, which allowed him to be seen on deck without being recognised. It was also his job to procure the food from the local shops, and as his wife forbade him from eating anything high in cholesterol, he had chosen everything he had missed in the last five years.

'This is the first chance I've had in the last two years to eat what I want, and I plan to make the most of it,' Levine said.

'Why don't you just tell your wife to cook you some decent food?' Avery asked.

'Because my wife doesn't ask me; she tells me. That's the way it is, has been and always will be.'

'Carl, I've met your wife and she's a pussycat,' Paul Bennett said. 'You keep banging on about her being some kind of monster, but whenever we get together, she's always been an absolute diamond.'

'Yeah, when you're with her, she plays the shy little girl, but once you're gone, she chews me a new arsehole for drinking three beers or eating anything containing a gram of fat.'

'Then cook something decent when she's at work,' Fletcher suggested.

'She can't work,' Carl said, 'not with what she's got.'

'What has she got?' Fletcher asked solemnly, thinking he must have missed some recent news.

'A lazy fucking disposition,' Carl said deadpan, bringing chuckles from the others.

'I can't believe you're scared of a woman,' Sonny snorted. 'If she's always whining, why don't you leave her?'

'For the same reason we don't leave you for whining about the food and why we don't moan when you snore all night,' Carl said from the dining table. 'Speaking of food, where are my sausages?'

Barker-Fink brought the pile of sandwiches over, and all eight men added their choice of condiments before wolfing them down.

Sonny nudged Len Smart, distracting him from his Kindle.

'What you reading, bookworm?'

'*Fatal Exchange* by Russell Blake. It's about a hot female bike messenger.'

'Sounds corny,' Sonny smirked.

'Stunning would be more accurate,' Smart said, returning his attention to the book. 'Besides, she'd kick your sorry ass.'

'I could murder a beer,' Michael Fletcher said to no one in particular.

'Patience, laddie,' Levine said. 'A couple more days and you'll get your piss-up.'

* * *

At eight thirty on the dot, Tom Gray sat in front of the webcam and started the video stream. 'Ladies and gentlemen, thank you for joining me. I have the results for Adrian Harper.'

As with the previous day, he checked the values shown on the website as well as the values sent through his other software. After a moment tapping at the keyboard, he looked into the camera.

'As you can see from the results which have just appeared on your screen, the majority of the votes are to free Adrian.' He stood up and walked over to the cell holding the second prisoner. After standing in the doorway for a moment, staring at the teenager, he stepped back and closed the door, before returning to the camera.

'Adrian will be allowed to leave here on Thursday. The people of Britain have voted, and I have found no discrepancies, so I will honour your wishes.' After more tapping on the keyboard, he addressed the camera one last time. 'Tomorrow it is the turn of Joseph Olemwu to learn his fate. Joseph is nineteen years old and has a criminal record stretching back seven years. His speciality is street robbery, but he also has convictions for burglary, assault and possession of a class A drug with intent to supply.

'You, the people of Britain, have already shown that you are unwilling to sentence a man to death. That is understandable, and it is why you have to think carefully about your next choice.' Gray held up a weapon and showed it to the camera. There were six thin branches, bound together at the handle. There was more binding up to the halfway point, with the remaining twenty inches allowed to flex independently. 'If you think Joseph has had all of his chances, vote "Die" to the usual email address shown on your screen. If you think he just deserves to be birched, vote "Live".

If you don't think he deserves either of these punishments, *do not vote*. This will give a true indication of how the people of Britain feel. I also urge you to vote on my justice bill. You can download a copy from this website, using the link at the top of the page. Voting on the bill closes at eleven thirty tomorrow morning, so don't hang around.'

When the transmission ended, Andrew Harvey closed down the browser and turned to his team. 'We got lucky today, people, but tomorrow a kid is either going to get birched or shot. Diane, we need that device. He used his position within his old company to gain access to Norden Industries, so maybe he also used that position to gain access to wherever he planted it. Go through his company records to see which businesses he has provided advice to, then search them all.' Harvey turned to Farsi. 'Hamad, Gray's last visit to Norden Industries was the seventh of March. I want you to put all CCTV from his last address and a fifteen-mile radius through facial recognition and see if we can follow a trail. Take it from that date, and use who you need from the training pool to do the same for the other major cities. We need to know everywhere he's been in the last forty days.'

Farsi scratched the back of his head. 'That's a huge task, Andrew. There must be millions of hours of CCTV to go through.'

'I know, I know, but we need something—anything—to get a lead on where he planted that device. Our second priority is finding those who helped him. What's the latest?'

'I passed the assignment to Special Branch as you asked, and they'll be asking plod to make enquiries. They have recent photos of all eight men, and local forces will be going to all B&Bs in their own districts. Do you want me to pass it to the media, too?'

Harvey thought for a moment. 'Do it. Tell them these people are not to be approached; we just want information on their whereabouts. Diane, get on to GCHQ and ask them if they can trace any signals going into Gray's location. If someone calls him, can we identify the source?'

Lane nodded and went to make the enquiry. She returned a few minutes later to inform him that it could be done.

Harvey thanked her and went to share an idea with his boss. He knocked on Hammond's door and waited to be called in. 'My plan,' he said, 'is to give the mug shots to the media, and after a few hours we release a statement saying we have arrested these men. Hopefully this will either get Gray to contact them or one of them to contact him.'

'Or let Gray know that we are desperate,' Hammond offered.

'And he'd be right, but I was thinking of giving them time to contact each other and then releasing a statement saying it was mistaken identity. He must appreciate that that kind of thing might happen, especially with the whole country on alert.'

'Okay,' Hammond said after a moment, 'release the details to the media, and announce the arrests four hours after it goes out. Give it another three hours, and say it was a mistake. If they haven't been in touch with each other by then, they are unlikely to fall for it. It's getting late, so release the pictures to the media now, but leave the arrest announcement until the morning when they are more likely to see it.'

Harvey nodded and left to pass on the instructions. At his desk he found several updates on the internal messaging system, and he flicked through them, assigning them to the relevant operatives, annotating them with his own notes and instructions. He was coming towards the end of the list when one particular name caused him to search his memory.

Abdul Mansour.

He knew the name but couldn't quite place it, so he searched for his file and brought up the summary page.

Abdul Mansour was listed as having been responsible for training a terrorist cell which was smashed in 2009. The cell had been planning an attack on a shopping centre in the capital, using Heckler and Koch MP-5K machine pistols and dozens of homemade pipe bombs, but unwittingly they had taken an MI5 operative into their fold. Two of the terrorists had travelled to Pakistan to one of the many training camps located near the Afghanistan border, and on their return they'd mentioned that they had met Mansour. He had been unknown to MI5 prior to their visit, but by their accounts he was an up-and-coming figure in the Taliban. It was Mansour who had led their training, and he had possessed an extensive knowledge of London, leading the security services to wonder if he was actually a British national.

Their investigations led them to conclude that Mansour was in fact Ahmed Al-Ali, a student from Ladbroke Grove. His parents had arrived in the UK from Pakistan in the late eighties, and Ahmed was born a year after they were naturalised as British citizens.

Al-Ali had been a bright student with good grades. As a teenager he had been spotted on several antiwar protests and was known to frequent a mosque the security services had taken an interest in. In 2007, he had boarded a flight to Pakistan, with minimal luggage, and that was the last that had been seen of him. Sources in Pakistan had no information on him, and it was only a few months later that Abdul Mansour came onto the scene.

His name first came up when a member of the Taliban was captured and interrogated by the CIA. Mansour had been seen with several other high-ranking members, and the description offered sounded a lot like Al-Ali, except he was now sporting a full beard. As was typical of the CIA, they decided to keep this information to themselves, and it wasn't until his name had been mentioned in

2009 that MI5 asked them for any information they had on him, and the link was made.

However, when the CIA reported Mansour as having been a victim of a drone attack in January 2010, in which several insurgents were killed just inside Afghanistan, his file had been closed. Now, it seemed, the facial recognition software at Heathrow airport had found an 80 percent match for Mansour based on his student ID photograph. The alert had been downgraded due to his current status—deceased—but had been recorded nonetheless.

Harvey passed an annotated version of the alert to the analysts, asking that it be passed to one of the juniors to see what they could find out about the passenger, a Pakistan national named Rahman Jamshed. It would probably come to nothing, but it was good experience for them.

He yawned and rubbed his eyes. A glance at his watch told him that he had arrived in the office over fourteen hours earlier. *Time to head home and get some rest*, he thought, although no matter how tired he was, he knew sleep would not come easily.

Chapter Twelve
Tuesday, 19 April 2011

Sally Clarkson turned on her computer and immediately took the novel from her handbag, opening it at the bookmark. The computer, like all others in the building, held her information in a central repository rather than on the local hard drive. This way, if her computer were corrupted or the hard drive failed, she would not lose any of her work. The downside of this was that it took around five minutes to load the security profile. and she used this time to catch up on her favourite detective series. She was just about to find out how Lester Stone was going to escape from the furnace when her computer beeped, announcing that it was ready for her user name and password.

Putting her book to one side, she entered her details and hit the 'Enter' key. A few moments later her profile appeared and she went straight to her email inbox. There were only three messages, none of which were of any importance. She then opened the internal messaging system and saw the message from Andrew Harvey.

Her heart began to race as she read the message and instructions: a real investigation at last. After eight months of learning the service processes and policies followed by filing, classifying and looking for trends in the volumes of available data, she was finally getting to do some real detective work.

Her love of crime stories had begun in her late teens, and her personal library of detective novels filled three shelves in her one-bedroom apartment. At the age of nineteen, she had applied to be a Metropolitan Police officer and had attended the one-day assessment at Hendon, but during one of the role-play scenarios, she had shown that she was easily intimidated and didn't have the ability to assert herself in pressure situations.

With her detective career over before it had begun, she had then turned her attentions to the Security Service, hoping to get a role as an intelligence officer, but her test scores had been slightly too low for that role. They were, however, good enough to qualify for an intelligence analyst position, and she had jumped at the chance.

She sat back and tried to steady her breathing.

Right, where do we begin? The airport, of course. Sally looked up the access page for immigration control and sifted through the entries for the previous day, filtering the results by flight departure point. Within seconds she had the entry for Jamshed, Rahman, and looked through the details. He had a six-month visitors' visa and had given his address as Green Street in Forest Gate, a largely Pakistani community.

Sally Clarkson printed out both the airport image and the image of Ahmed Al-Ali and put them in her bag. After checking that she had her smart phone, she locked her computer and headed downstairs to arrange her cover details.

The BBC News channel had been running pleas by the parents of two of Gray's remaining hostages for the previous twenty-four hours and it was beginning to bore him. Both sets of parents were saying the same thing: that their son was a good lad and didn't deserve any of this. *Yes, proper little saints,* Gray thought, as the sequence began again for the umpteenth time. However, once it had finished, the newscaster announced that the parents of the other boy, Joseph Olemwu, would be speaking to them live in the studio after the weather report.

Gray had a quick scan of the monitors, and satisfied that there would be no interruptions in the next few minutes, he sat back to watch, hoping for something more original from this family.

He wasn't disappointed.

The parents were introduced as Olefina Olemwu and Michael Vincent. The mother was in her late forties and had probably been quite a catch in her youth, but the years hadn't been kind to her. The father, in his fifties with a short white beard and shaven head, sat a good nine inches taller than her. It was clear from the outset that though the mother simply wanted her boy back, the father's only intention was to have a dig at the authorities.

'I want to know what the police are doing to rescue my boy,' was his opening statement, before he had even been asked a question.

'Mr Vincent, I'm sure the police are doing everything in their power to try and resolve this without loss of further life,' the newscaster said, before turning his attention to the mother. 'Mrs Olemwu, these must be terribly difficult times for you. What would you like to say to Tom Gray?'

'I want him to think about what he is doing. Joseph may not be an angel, but he is loved in the eyes of the Lord just as much as every other person on this planet. It is not for Tom Gray to play judge, jury and executioner: it is God who will guide Joseph onto the proper path.'

Before the newscaster had a chance to move on to the next question, the father continued his rant. 'The police are on Joseph's back day and night, but when this happens, they won't do anything. If he was a white kid with rich parents they would be storming that place by now, but because he is just a poor black kid from a council estate, they sit on their hands and do nothing.'

'Mr Vincent, if the police were to attack Tom Gray, it might well mean the deaths of thousands of innocent people,' the newscaster reminded him. 'I'm sure this has nothing to do with the colour of your son's skin or his background.'

'You say that, but if it was a white politician's son in there, they would have sent in the SAS, SWAT and God knows who else to get them out. The government just don't care about poor black people, and this proves it. They are going to sit back while the world watches my son die.' Olefina put a hand on her partner's arm to calm him down, but he shrugged it off. 'This man is a coward, but the government are scared of him. He doesn't even have the balls face up to his crimes.'

While the newscaster moved on quickly and the producer's voice reminded Vincent to watch his language, Gray smiled and turned on the prepaid mobile phone which had the BBC newsroom's number in the speed dial. Once the parents had had their four minutes in the limelight, he hit the button, asked for the producer and gave his code word. Within a minute he was live on air.

'Good morning, Mr Gray. I understand you are joining us to give your reaction to Mr Vincent's claims, is that correct?'

'That's right, Sharon. He surely will have noticed that there are five boys here, and only one is black. Therefore his claim that the police are doing nothing because of his son's colour has no merit.'

'I was actually referring to his claim that you are a coward.'

'Ah. I must admit I found that strange. I am showing my face to the nation, so everyone knows who I am. Does he think I should be braver, like his son, going around in a gang attacking and robbing innocent people, then running off to escape the consequences?'

'Mr Gray, I think he was referring to the fact that you intend to take your life when this is all over. Isn't that escaping the consequences, too?'

'In case you haven't noticed, Sharon, there is a global recession, and Britain didn't escape its effects. The ordinary working people of Britain are feeling this more than anyone, and I don't want to add insult to injury, if you'll pardon the pun, by taking part in a trial which could cost the ordinary taxpayer millions of pounds. This way is much simpler and a whole lot cheaper for the nation.'

The news anchor pressed the point. 'Couldn't you just plead guilty and avoid a trial, Mr Gray? Or don't you feel you are guilty of any crimes?'

'Far from it, Sharon. I know I am guilty and deserve to be punished, but once again we come back to the current justice system and the fact that I have been informed that I will face charges under the Terrorism Act. Firstly, I don't consider myself a terrorist and would fight those charges to the bitter end. Secondly, I will also be charged with murder, kidnapping, false imprisonment, assault and a variety of other charges, and even if I plead guilty to all of these charges, the sentences will probably run concurrently. This means that you take the largest penalty, and that is all I will serve. I might get thirty years for murder, twenty years for kidnapping, six years for assault, but the most I will serve is the thirty years for the murder.

'I'm sure you're familiar with the phrase "might as well hang for a sheep as a lamb". Well, most criminals have this mentality, and that is why they commit crime after crime. They know that once they have been caught, they can ask for all the other offences to be taken into consideration and their sentences will run concurrently, so they are effectively punished for the latest crime only. My justice bill will do away with this, so criminals will be punished for every crime they commit.'

'So you are saying that you would be willing to plead guilty to a single murder charge?'

'It's not as simple as that, Sharon. The current justice system wouldn't allow the prosecutor to pick and choose the charges I face. That's why it's either a full trial where I can contest some of the charges, or I end this as I have always intended, and I have already explained my unwillingness to add to this country's financial burden.'

'Moving on, Mr Gray, the police have given the names of eight people they want to question in connection with your activities. What can you tell me about these people?'

Gray had seen the announcement the previous evening, along with the mug shots of his friends. It hadn't been unexpected—just a little sooner than he had anticipated.

'I can tell you that I know these people, but I don't know why the police want to talk to them. They have nothing to do with this.'

'Have they been—'

'Sorry, Sharon, but I came on today to give my reaction to Mr Vincent's comment. I won't answer questions about these people as they have no connection with what I am doing.'

Gray cut the connection before she could start her next question. *Have I gotten my point across?* he wondered. Only time would tell.

Chapter Thirteen

Andrew Harvey had been at his desk since six that morning. As expected, sleep had been hard to come by, and after finally dropping off at three in the morning, he'd found himself awake just two hours later. After a quick shower, he had set off for the office, grabbing a strong coffee on the way.

As his colleagues began to drift in, he first asked Diane Lane to inform GCHQ to begin monitoring transmissions in and out of Gray's location, then reiterated his request for companies Gray had visited in the last six months. Lane brought the details over twenty minutes later, and he saw that there were twelve of them.

'Get this to Special Branch,' he told her.

'Already done. There's also a video from BBC News in the archives.'

'Gray?' he asked. He had checked the BBC News website earlier that morning, but it had contained nothing new. This must have happened recently.

'Yeah. Olemwu's father wound him up, and he wanted to have his say.'

Harvey found the file in the archives and played it twice. He was hoping that Gray would sound tense, under pressure, losing the plot, but he still seemed as calm and in control as ever. However, it was what he said, rather than the way he said it, that grabbed him.

When John Hammond arrived, Harvey followed him into his office and threw his idea at him.

'I'll have to put it to the home secretary,' Hammond told him, 'but it is all conditional on finding those eight men.'

Harvey nodded his understanding and left to speak to Special Branch, asking them to place the call to the BBC. He brought up the BBC News website on his computer, and within ten minutes the article appeared next to the 'Breaking News' icon:

> *Reports are coming in that eight men, believed to be the associates of Tom Gray, have been arrested. The men were taken to separate police stations in London and will be quizzed in connection with the abduction of the five men being held by Tom Gray.*
>
> *Police have revealed no further details at this time.*

John Hammond appeared at Harvey's desk. 'The home secretary has agreed to our suggestion. He wasn't happy, of course, and it's conditional on it happening before anyone else dies.'

'Fair enough. I guess another death would make it difficult for him to justify his decision.'

Hammond returned to his office, and Harvey busied himself as he waited for the call from GCHQ.

Sally Clarkson drove past the address in Green Street and saw that it was a flat above a clothes shop. She drove on in search of a parking space, but these were at a premium, so she pulled into a residential side street and parked outside a semi-detached house. Walking back to the main road, she tried to control her breathing. *Easy, girl. All you have to do is knock on the door, ask to see Mr Jamshed and ask him a simple question.*

Try as she might, her pulse continued to race, so she found a newsagent and bought a pack of cigarettes and a lighter. Outside the shop she ripped the nicotine patch off her arm, fumbled with the cellophane wrapper on the pack and pulled one out. The first deep drag hit her instantly, making her feel lightheaded, and she cursed herself for giving in after three weeks of abstinence. Nevertheless, she smoked the rest of the cigarette and stubbed it out on the pavement. Her pulse was still racing as a result of the nicotine hit, but she felt much more in control, so she made her way to the address.

There was no access from the main street, so she continued along the street until she came to an alleyway leading to the rear of the building. Here she found four kids playing a game that looked like a combination of football and cricket, using an old fruit crate as the wickets. They paused their game as she walked past but were quickly back into their swing as she walked towards the correct building.

She rang the bell and waited for an answer. After a minute she tried again and was rewarded with the sound of movement behind the door. It was answered by a man wearing shoulder-length dreadlocks.

'Hello,' Sally said, flashing her ID and a smile, 'I'm Sarah Clark from the UK Border Agency. Would it be possible to speak to Mr Rahman Jamshed?'

Her cover name used the same initials as her real name—and was quite similar—in order for it to be easier to remember.

The man looked at her ID card and shook his head. 'You've got the wrong address, lady. There's just me and my daughter, and there's barely room for us two, never mind anyone else.'

Sally didn't doubt him: she thought it unlikely that a Pakistan national and a Rastafarian would share accommodation. Which meant that, for whatever reason, Rahman Jamshed had given a false address when he passed through immigration at Heathrow, and that made her heart skip a beat.

After apologising to the occupant for wasting his time, she returned to her car, smoking another cigarette on the way. The ten-mile drive back to Thames House took well over an hour, but it gave her time to plan her strategy.

Her first step was to pull up the CCTV for the arrivals area of Heathrow airport at the time of Rahman Jamshed's arrival. She found him as he walked purposefully through the arrivals lounge towards the exit. Switching to the outside camera, she watched him get into a black cab and zoomed in to get the licence plate. After noting it down, she got onto the Police National Computer and brought up the owner's details. Armed with his name and address, she finally searched the database for his details and got a mobile number, which she called.

'Hello,' a cheery voice said.

'Hello, Mr Watkins? My name is Sarah, and I'm calling from the UK Border Agency. I understand you took a fare from Heathrow yesterday at around two in the afternoon.'

'That's right, an Indian guy. I took him to Kilburn Park tube station.'

'Do you know if he went into the tube station, Mr Wilkins?'

'Sorry, darling, once they've paid and gone, I take no notice.'

Sally thanked him and hung up. Although Kilburn was predominately an Irish community, there were also Indian, Bangladeshi and Pakistani communities in the area, too. Had he gone into the station, or was he staying in the area? She pulled up the CCTV for the entrance to Kilburn Station and opened her packed lunch, knowing that this could be a long day.

Tom Gray was momentarily taken aback when the news anchor announced the arrests of his friends. It had come totally out of the blue, and he spent a few minutes considering the implications before coming to the conclusion that it wouldn't affect his plans too much. Having said that, if they had been caught, what had they done to give themselves away? Had they stuck to the mission and the police had just gotten lucky, or had his friends been careless?

Andrew Harvey would be in touch, of that there was no doubt, but how should he deal with it? He spent fifteen minutes running the possible conversation in his head before turning his mobile phone on and sitting back to await the call.

But after twenty minutes, none came. He checked the phone in case it wasn't working, but he had a good signal and the battery was fully charged. Should he initiate the call? *No, just wait it out.*

After another hour had passed, he found himself pacing around the room. Why hadn't Harvey called? Was he waiting to verify their identities? Did he want to speak to them before he called? Had they escaped? No, if they had escaped, they would . . .

He slapped himself on the forehead and went to the laptop, bringing up the dead-drop email account and signing in. Both he and his friends had the user name and password to this free account, and it had been set up four months ago, using false details. A few emails had been sent to various websites asking for information, not because they were pertinent but simply to keep the account from lapsing. Since Sunday afternoon they had created dead-drop emails every eight hours to stay in touch, but rather than sending them to each other and creating a trail, the emails were saved as drafts. His friends would save a draft with 'Many' as the subject, and Tom would read it before discarding it. When Tom wrote a draft he would use 'One' as the subject.

Tom had read the last draft email from them at eight that morning, and it had contained the code word that told him everything was okay: 'Furniture'. If he had read 'Bathroom', he would have known something was amiss. When he signed in now, he found a draft which had been saved forty minutes earlier. He opened it and read the message:

'Furniture—what's going on? It isn't us.'

Gray discarded the draft and created one of his own:

'Furniture—proceed as planned.'

He saved the draft and signed out, relieved that they were sticking to operational procedures, but unhappy at Harvey's subterfuge. Unhappy, though not surprised, and he realised he could turn this to his advantage. He called Harvey's mobile, and it picked up on the second ring.

'Hello, Andrew.'

'Tom. How can I help you?'

'I understand you are holding some friends of mine,' Gray said.

'Not us, Tom. Special Branch.'

'Why were they arrested? What are they supposed to have done?'

'You know what they did, Tom. We have an eyewitness from the Olemwu kidnapping who placed Simon Baines at the scene, and we're waiting to interview another witness to Mark Smith's abduction. We know there's no way you could have done this alone.'

Gray remained silent for a few moments, then said, 'So what happens to them now?'

'Simple. They'll be charged with aiding and abetting, kidnapping, false imprisonment, assault and any other charges that come to light during their interviews. That's before we even get to the offences under the Terrorism Act.'

'I coerced them,' Gray said lamely.

'Sorry, Tom, that won't wash. Even if I believed you, you couldn't explain that in court, as you will be dead by the time it goes to trial. I'm afraid they will have to take their own chances and live with the consequences, as will their families.' As he spoke the last words, Harvey hoped they had the desired effect. There was a noticeable pause before Gray responded.

'I want you to let them go, Andrew. Release them and give me assurances that they will never be charged. I've lost my family; they don't deserve to lose theirs.'

'If you end this now, agree to come out and give us the location of the device, I'll see what I can do.'

'Andrew, if you look through my justice bill, you will see that at every stage I am raising revenue to allow more policing, so I am not going to waste a couple of million pounds of taxpayer's money on a trial.'

'What if I can guarantee that the only charge you will be faced with is murder?'

There was another pause before Gray asked, 'I only face murder and my friends go free? No charges, ever?'

'I can't guarantee that there will be no charges for your friends. They might have to face a token charge just to placate the families of the boys you are holding.'

'I'll think about it and get back to you.'

Gray ended the call and turned the phone off, the beginnings of a smile on his face. A glance at his watch told him he had a few minutes before it was time to announce the result of the justice bill, so he checked the monitors for signs of anything out of the ordinary. What he saw was that the black Land Rover had returned, and climbing out of the driver's side was Sergeant Todd Dennis.

The sight of Todd was a welcome one. A solid NCO, Gray had been his squad leader in Iraq and had been most impressed with his attention to detail and his knack of making the right decision, especially under pressure. That same man was now tasked with finding a way through his defences, and it was reassuring to know that he was not one for taking unnecessary risks.

With nothing else requiring his immediate attention, he turned to his laptop to check the results. As had been the trend over the last twenty-four hours, the people were overwhelmingly in favour of a referendum, and he prepared the webcam to share the news.

'Ladies and gentlemen, thank you for joining me today. As you can see from the figures on your screens, the vast majority of you, over 70 percent, are unhappy with the current justice system and want the government to implement my justice bill.

'This, however, is just the first step. You, the public, have told the government what you want, and it is now up to them to decide if they want to listen to you. They may choose to ignore your voice, or they may, with an election looming, choose to give the people what they want by promising to hold a full referendum on Thursday, the third of May, next year.

'To the government I say, make your choice wisely. If you agree to a referendum and renege once this is over, you will be showing the people that you cannot be trusted. You can, of course, choose to refuse a referendum, in which case you will be showing the people that you are happy with the way criminals and their victims are being treated. I don't want you to make your decision to try and placate me; that is not what this is about. It is about whether or not you are willing to listen to the voice of the people.

'Prime Minister, you have had plenty of time to read through the bill and seek the opinions of your advisors. However, I will give you another twenty-four hours to let the nation know your decision. I would like an announcement to be made at midday tomorrow on the BBC News channel.

'I will be back at the usual time this evening with the results of the votes for Joseph Olemwu.'

Gray turned off the webcam, and after checking the monitors again, he prepared lunch for his guests. When he removed the tape from Olemwu's mouth, the boy immediately began pleading with him.

'Man, you gotta let me go. My arms and legs are killin' me. I'm gonna get deep vein frombosis or somfin'.'

'That's the least of your worries,' Gray told him. 'It's your turn tonight.'

'Look, I don't wanna die, man. All I did was nick a few phones and shit. You can't kill me for that.'

'It's not up to me. It's up to all the people who have had their phones nicked by little shits like you.'

'That's bullshit!' Olemwu spat, showing his true colours. 'You'll be the one pulling the trigger, so it's your fuckin' choice.'

Gray seemed to consider the statement for a moment before replying. 'You're right, I suppose. Even if they vote for you to die, I still have the choice of either pulling the trigger or not. I have the chance to do the right thing because I am the one who has to live with the consequences.'

'That's right,' Olemwu said, beginning to glimpse hope. 'You can do the right thing, man.'

Gray rubbed his chin and feigned contemplation. After a while he said, 'Hmmm. Let me ask you something. When you went to court for the first time, did they send you to prison?'

'No, man, they just gave me a fine and a curfew.'

'And did you obey the curfew and stop "nickin' phones and shit"?' Gray asked, mimicking the boy's accent.

Olemwu hesitated with his answer. 'No, I—'

'No,' Gray interrupted, 'you had a choice between taking your punishment and going straight, or carrying on with your old ways, and you chose to break the curfew and continue mugging people. So why should I change my ways when you weren't prepared to change yours?'

Olemwu again struggled for an answer. Gray gave him five seconds to come up with one, but when nothing was forthcoming he ripped off a new piece of tape and put it over the boy's mouth. 'It's not all your fault, Joseph. If the courts hadn't been so lenient, you might not be here now. However, you *are* here and must face the consequences, just as I will. In the meantime, it won't hurt you to miss a meal. Somehow I always think better on an empty stomach; let's see if it works for you.'

He wheeled the trolley into the next cell and prepared to remove the tape from Mark Smith's mouth. 'You say one word, the tape goes back on and you starve. Understand?'

The youth nodded his head and Gray ripped the tape off, taking a little of his fledgling moustache with it. Smith began to curse but held his tongue when Gray gave him a stern look. The trolley was wheeled up to Smith's chest and a straw placed in the glass of water, and Gray moved on to Stuart Boyle.

'Not a word,' Gray warned him, and ripped off the tape.

'Mister, I'm sorry—'

Gray's balled fist was a blur, and it caught Boyle on the side of his right eye, just below the temple. The boy went limp and Gray put a new piece of tape over his mouth.

'You never fucking learn,' he said, wheeling the trolley out of the cell.

With lunch served, Gray turned his phone on and called Harvey.

'Hello, Andrew.'

'Tom. Have you made your decision?'

'Yes, I have. I have decided that as I have just heard from my friends, you were lying to me, and therefore I can't trust you, so the deal is off.'

Harvey was confused. He had heard nothing from GCHQ, so how could they have been in touch? Email? Unlikely, as they were monitoring all incoming traffic through his Internet Service Provider. *It must be a dead-drop email. Damn! How could they not have thought of that?*

'We must have the wrong guys, then,' he offered, trying to sound as apologetic as possible.

'Don't insult me, Andrew. You tried to suck them out, and it didn't work. I don't like it when you treat me like an idiot.'

Harvey held his mobile to his chest as he thought of a reply. 'I'm sorry, Tom. However, the offer still stands. We are going to catch them sooner or later, and they are going to face some pretty stiff charges.'

'No, they aren't, Andrew. Your little stunt has raised the stakes, so if you want me to come in, you get me a guarantee that they face no charges whatsoever.'

'I'll see—'

'Also,' Gray interrupted, 'I want the home secretary to go live on TV and announce the amnesty. I only face a charge of murder, and they face no charges whatsoever. I also want it to stipulate that we will never face any civil charges, whether filed by these boys or their families. The home secretary has to have a copy of the agreement delivered here to me, and a duplicate delivered to the BBC so that they can show it and its contents. I won't have him going back on his word.'

'We can make that request, but we can't tell him what to do, Tom. You have to understand that.'

'Finally, I am going to put this to the public and let them vote on it.'

'Tom, there's no need—'

'In the meantime, anything I do to these boys between now and the time I come out has no bearing on the agreement. If the public vote for Olemwu to die, he will die. If they vote for him to be birched, he will be birched.'

'You're asking a lot, Tom.'

'That's what happens when you piss me off. Just think yourself lucky that the rest are still alive after your little stunt.'

The phone went dead, and Harvey cursed to himself as he marched to Hammond's office.

'John, I just spoke to Gray,' he told his boss. Hammond sat silent as Harvey went over the conversation, and couldn't hide his disappointment when his subordinate had finished.

'The home secretary is going to have a conniption fit,' he finally said. 'How the hell could you forget a dead-drop email?'

'I underestimated him,' Harvey admitted sheepishly.

Hammond glared at him. Eventually his demeanour mellowed. 'At least he has gone for the offer, even if it does have caveats. I just have the simple task of squaring it with the home secretary.'

As he picked up the phone, he gestured with his head for Harvey to leave the room. Harvey was only too happy to oblige. He went to his desk and called Simon Crawford at Norden Industries. Although it was possible that the home secretary would agree to Gray's conditions, it would be preferable to find the device first. If not find it, then at least identify it.

'Mr Crawford, anything to report?'

'Not yet, Mr Harvey. So far we have checked over four thousand canisters but everything is in order. We have three shifts working around the clock and my bosses are not happy about the expenditure.'

'Then you should point out that if they hadn't scrimped in the beginning, we wouldn't be doing this. Four thousand canisters a day is not enough, Mr Crawford. Is there any way you can intensify the search?'

'I'm afraid not, Mr Harvey. It's not a case of personnel, but the facilities to check the contents of the canisters. We simply can't process any more canisters than we currently are.'

'What about spreading the load around other facilities?' Harvey asked.

'There are no other facilities that can handle these compounds. Unless we consider private facilities ... ' He left the question hanging, but Harvey dismissed the idea.

'No, we can't have this going public. Just get back to me if you have any news.'

He cut the connection and went to see Gerald Small.

'Any hits from the CCTV?' he asked the technician.

'Nothing yet,' Small told him.

'How far have you got?'

'We're doing quite well, actually. I have created virtual machines and loaded an instance of the facial recognition software on each. This lets us divide the work up between the twelve instances, so we are scanning a dozen times faster than we normally would. However, there are a lot of images to go through.'

'Can't you make more virtual machines?' Harvey asked.

'Not that simple, I'm afraid. It's a case of processor power, and we are near the maximum as it is. Any more and the whole lot will crash.'

Harvey wasn't about to second-guess the expert, so he took his leave and went to speak to Special Branch. He had just instructed them to release the statement announcing that they had arrested the wrong people when Hammond summoned him into his office.

'Well, I can't say that was the most pleasant conversation I've ever had,' Hammond said. 'An election around the corner, and there I was asking him to commit political suicide.'

'Did he agree to it?'

'Yes, reluctantly, and at a cost. He made it quite clear that heads will roll when this is over. Yours and mine for a start. He also wants us to try and get a hostage freed as a show of good faith.' Hammond sat back in his chair, rubbing his temple. It was a while before he spoke again.

'The deal only stands once Gray agrees to it. We have until then to find an alternative resolution that will save our necks. What progress are we making?'

'Gerald is working hard on tracking Gray's movements in the hours and days following his visit to Norden Industries. If we can follow his tracks, we might be able to locate the device. There's little point in using police resources to look for his friends now, so we can concentrate them on searching the most likely targets.'

Hammond wrung his hands, looking around the room as if for inspiration. 'The boys from Hereford say the only way in is to introduce a sleeping agent into the building and move in when it takes effect. However, the chances of being discovered while they try to introduce it are extremely high, given his CCTV coverage. Even if they did manage to deliver it, Gray has been well trained in resisting interrogation, and chances are he could hold out long enough for the device to go off. That leaves finding the device as our only option.

'As the deal isn't valid until Gray accepts it, we take advantage of that. We need to find his friends, and we squeeze them for every bit of information they have. Gloves off, if you get my meaning.'

Harvey nodded his understanding and left Hammond's office, pulling out his mobile. He thumbed through his recent numbers and called Gray. 'Hello, Tom.'

'Andrew. What did the home secretary say?'

'He has agreed to your demands, Tom. He will provide immunity from prosecution for your friends, and you will only face the charge of murder. The deal is valid once you accept it.'

He paused a moment, considering the best way to phrase the next request. 'There is a condition, Tom. He wants you to free a hostage, to give him some political leverage.'

'Well, that's up to the public. I'd better go and let them know. In the meantime, I want you to deliver the agreement personally. I'll see you in four hours.'

'We need a decision about the hostage now, Tom; otherwise, the deal is off. His words, not mine.'

Gray hesitated for what seemed to Harvey an interminable time. 'Okay, you can have one. I will send him out in the next ten minutes, but he has to learn a lesson before he leaves.'

'Tom, don't do anything—'

The phone went dead, and Harvey put it back in his pocket before sitting at his desk and putting his head in his hands. Sally Clarkson came up and stood next to him, waiting patiently for him to notice her, but he was in a world of his own, so she gave a little cough to grab his attention.

'Hi. Andrew Harvey?'

'Yes.'

'I'm Sally from downstairs.'

This meant nothing to Harvey, and his look said as much, so she explained the purpose of her visit. 'Sorry. I was assigned the Rahman Jamshed case. I've found something. Well, it might be something, it might be nothing, but, um, well, it seems like he might be up to something.'

Harvey grabbed his jacket and put it on. 'I'm sorry, Sally, but I haven't got time for this. Just send me a summary, and I'll get back to you.'

He headed for the exit, desperate for some fresh air and a chance to clear his head.

'But Mr Harvey—'

'Enough!' Harvey shouted, grabbing the attention of the entire room. All eyes upon him, he put his hands up in apology. He thought for a second of explaining himself, but instead he turned and left the office, the beginnings of a headache forming at the base of his skull.

Chapter Fourteen

Tom Gray dialled the number for the BBC News producer and told him about the latest developments. Within ten minutes he was once again the main story.

'We're hearing about startling developments in the Tom Gray saga,' the news anchor told her audience. 'Mr Gray has just informed us that the home secretary has agreed to offer immunity from prosecution for all those accused of helping him in his venture. In addition, Mr Gray has been told that he will only face a single murder charge if he hands himself in and reveals the location of his bomb. In return, Mr Gray has agreed to release a hostage. At this moment in time, we do not know which one it will be, but we will bring that to you as soon as possible.

'We hope to speak to a Home Office spokesperson shortly to see if we can get more details about the agreement. We will also be speaking to our Home Affairs correspondent, John Lythe. Join us again after the weather and news from where you are.'

As the announcement was made, there was a lot of backslapping and a few high fives on board a narrow boat in Norfolk. One or two wanted to go and grab a few beers to celebrate, but Len Smart, always the voice of reason, put paid to that idea.

'Let's see what they have to say,' he told them. 'Tris, drop Tom an email, see if this is just another ruse.'

Tristram Barker-Fink logged into the email account and saw no new messages, so he prepared a draft, saved it and logged out. 'He isn't due to check for another three hours, but if this is another wind up, Tom will let us know. I'll keep checking every fifteen minutes.'

They all gathered round the small TV and cranked up the sound. After enduring the local travel news and a piece on a local farmer's albino lamb, the focus returned to the main studio.

'You're watching the BBC News at one o'clock. The main headlines: The home secretary is prepared to offer immunity from prosecution if Tom Gray gives himself up; three NATO soldiers are killed in Sierra Leone as tensions rise; and fuel prices are set to rise as the budget kicks in.

'But first to our main story. The home secretary has offered immunity from prosecution for the eight people alleged to have been involved in the abductions of Tom Gray's hostages. He has also offered to disregard all charges against Tom Gray with the exception of a murder charge relating to the death of Simon Arkin. In return, Tom Gray has agreed to release one hostage immediately. We don't know who that will be but will keep you updated on that development.

'The home secretary is in our London studio. Home Secretary, thank you for joining us today. Can you explain the reasoning behind this offer?'

The minister appeared on a large screen off to the anchor's right. 'Hello. The reason I made this offer is to avoid any further loss of life, plain and simple. I have personally negotiated the release of one of the hostages, and Mr Gray has agreed to hand himself in to the authorities if I can guarantee that these eight individuals face no charges. I have looked at their service records, and they have served their country proudly in hostile conflicts around the world. I can understand their allegiance to Mr Gray, however misguided, and have agreed to his request that no charges will be brought against them.

'In terms of Tom Gray himself, I feel it necessary that he face the courts in order to restore faith in our judicial system. I have listened to Mr Gray's arguments that an expensive trial would not be in the public's best interest and his insistence that he would fight any charges under the Terrorism Act. Having weighed this up, I decided to make the offer so that he could be brought to justice.'

'Which hostage will he be releasing?'

'That we don't know, but we expect it to happen in the next few minutes.'

'How do you balance your decision with the government's policy of not negotiating with terrorists?' the anchor asked.

The home secretary, already briefed on the questions he would be asked, gave the prepared reply. 'We stand by our policy of not negotiating with terrorists. In this particular case we are not giving in to his demands and letting him go; we have achieved a situation whereby Mr Gray will be handing himself in and facing the consequences of his actions.'

'Will Mr Gray be handing himself in immediately?'

'That was our initial request, but Mr Gray informed us that he would like the people of Britain to make the decision. I therefore expect he will be making an announcement on his website in the near future.'

'But what if he were to harm or kill another of his hostages in the meantime? How would that affect the agreement?'

'The agreement does not come into force until Mr Gray accepts it. Until he does that, we will concentrate all of our resources in resolving this without injury or further loss of life. With this in mind, I urge the people of Britain to abstain from voting on the fate of Joseph Olemwu and the other boys being held by Mr Gray.'

'It sounds, Home Secretary, like you have given him carte blanche to do as he pleases with Joseph Olemwu.'

'That couldn't be farther from the truth, Sharon. If I hadn't made this offer to Mr Gray, we would be in the same situation as we find ourselves now, but I am confident that this agreement can end matters early, and justice will be seen to be done.'

'One final question, Home Secretary. Will you be releasing a copy of this agreement to the media?'

'Yes, a copy will be made available within the hour.'

'Home Secretary, thank you for joining us today.'

As the news anchor moved onto the next story after promising more on those developments, Len Smart reiterated his stance. 'Sounds like the real deal, but we wait to hear from Tom before we do anything.'

They kept one eye on the news channel, waiting for news of Tom's announcement, while his website was loaded on the laptops. After seven minutes the website performed an auto-refresh, and the video was ready to stream. Tristram Barker-Fink hit the 'Play' button and sat back so the others could crowd round.

'Ladies and gentlemen, the home secretary has made me an offer, and I want to once again put it to the people. The offer is to grant immunity from prosecution for the eight men accused—and I stress "accused"—of helping me in this week's events, if I turn myself in. In addition, I would only face a single charge of murder carrying a full life sentence, meaning I would face no charges under the Terrorism Act and avoid a lengthy and expensive trial.

'These eight men are indeed friends of mine. I have known them for many years and feel confident that a jury would find them not guilty of any charges they are likely to face. However, a trial would not only be an ordeal for them and their families, it would also damage the reputation of our beloved regiment.

'I said at the start of the week that I would take my own life when this was over, as I have already lost my family. However, in order to protect the families of my friends, I will entertain the home secretary's offer while leaving the final decision to you, the people of Britain.

'If you think I should hand myself in, send an email with Adrian as the subject and 'Live' in the body of the message. If you think I should refuse the offer and take my own life on Thursday, replace "Live" with "Die."

'When I started this venture, I only had the software set up for six rounds of votes: one for each of the boys and one for the justice bill. In order to allow you to vote on my fate, I will be releasing Adrian Harper, which is why you must put his name in the subject of the email, not mine.

'Voting starts now and ends at six o'clock tomorrow evening. I will reveal the results an hour later.'

The video ended and Michael Fletcher got up to stretch his legs. 'Whose turn is it to cook?'

'Yours,' the others chorused.

Tom Gray phoned his solicitor, Ryan Amos, and asked him to take a look at the agreement, just to ensure that it was genuine and covered the points the home secretary had promised. Amos was only too willing to help, having grown close to Gray and his family over the past four years. Tom faxed the document to him and received a call within five minutes to say it was genuine.

'Just to make sure, Ryan, I will only be charged with the murder of Simon Arkin and that's it?'

'Yep, just the one murder charge relating to the death of Simon Arkin, that's what it says.'

'And the eight men named on the document will never face any charges relating to what went on in the last two weeks?'

'None whatsoever,' Amos confirmed.

'What about any civil proceedings against any of us?'

'There won't be any, according to this.'

'Great. Thanks for your help, Ryan.'

'Tom, wait. You are going to need help when this is over. Do you want me to be there when you come out?'

'The public haven't voted yet, Ryan. I may not make it out at all,' Gray reminded him. 'If I do come out, though, then yes, I would like you to be here with that copy of the agreement. As you can see, I've already signed it, just in case. Will that be a valid document in a court?'

'Yes, if you give yourself up before the deadline of seven tomorrow evening, it will be.'

'Okay,' Gray said, 'I'll give you a ring tomorrow. Bye, Ryan, and thanks for everything.'

Gray hung up the phone and picked up a small sack before entering Adrian Harper's cell. The boy had been dozing but lifted his head at the sounds of the door opening, squinting against the light which invaded the dark room.

'Time to go home,' Gray said, as he covered the boy's head with the dark cloth bag. 'I'm going to untie you now. If you make any sudden moves, I'll stab you through the heart. Do you understand?'

Harper nodded like a jack-in-the-box in an earthquake and Gray removed the shackles from his feet and the ropes from his wrists. Harper let out a moan as his hands fell to his sides for the first time in days, his triceps burning in protest at the slightest movement.

'Get up,' Gray said, and he watched as Harper tried and failed to stand on his own two feet. His legs collapsed beneath him, and he lay on the floor, whimpering. Gray grabbed him under the armpits and lifted him to a standing position, dragging him towards the exit.

'Hold on here,' he said, and moved Harper's hands to the frame of the cell door. 'If you let go, I'll leave you where you drop and you stay in here.'

Harper gripped the wood with all of his might, summoning every last ounce of strength to keep himself upright. When he'd been committing a burglary or evading the police in a stolen car, he'd had a heightened sense of not fear, but excitement—the thrill of the prospect of being caught. This was totally different; this was fear he had never known, the knowledge that his very life was at risk, not just his liberty.

As Gray had expected, Harper gripped the frame but swung up against the inner wall of the cell in order to support his own weight. Seizing the moment, Gray grabbed the heavy door and slammed it closed on Harper's hands.

The boy collapsed to the floor, his screams muffled by the tape over his mouth.

'Oh, sorry,' Gray said, not even trying to sound apologetic. 'Let me help you.'

He took hold of Harper's hands and, ignoring his protestations, began dragging him towards the entrance to the building.

'I guess you won't be able to break into any homes for a while. Too bad. Still, it gives you time to reflect on what happened here this week.'

He didn't know if the boy was even listening, but as he reached the inner door, he let go of Harper's hands and grabbed his head, putting his mouth close to the boy's ear.

'This is your last chance to go straight, so don't waste it. The law is going to change, and you don't want to be on the wrong side of it.'

In order to leave the building, they had to go through two doors. Gray had built a wall around the inside of the main entrance, so anyone who made it through the front door would find themselves in a room only four feet deep and ten feet wide, with a sturdy door off to the left. It was secured from the inside by a metal bar which lay inside four strong brackets, two on the door itself and one on the frame each side.

He lifted the bar out, struggling slightly with the weight. It certainly wasn't going to be knocked out of place from the outside;

he was sure of that. After dragging Harper through the inner door, again ignoring the muffled screams, he looked at a small screen on the wall which showed a picture of the exterior. There was no sign of anyone lying in wait for him, not that he expected them to.

This door had the same locking mechanism as the inner door, and both opened outwards. This made it doubly difficult for anyone on the outside trying to break it down. He removed the steel bar and pushed the door open, taking in a deep breath. All his preparation, all his planning over the last six months, and he hadn't taken into account the stink of shit and piss that would invade every inch of the building. Chemical toilets would have eliminated the odour better than the wooden boxes they had been sitting on, but then it must have been a lot worse for them than it was for him, sitting atop the excrement all day long in a cell whose door was hardly ever opened. No, it was better this way. He just wished he'd thought to bring a can of air freshener.

With one last tug he pulled Harper into the daylight and left him lying on the concrete path. 'Don't move. Someone will come and collect you in a minute. If you roll off to either side, you will land on top of a mine, and that would be a shitty end to your day.'

Looking towards the command vehicle, he saw four men making their way towards him, arms outstretched to show they weren't armed. When they got within fifty yards, Gray told them to stop and do a three-sixty to see if they had any concealed weapons, but there were none. He motioned for them to continue and closed the door, reinserting the steel bar. On the screen he watched as they each grabbed a limb and carried the boy clear of the building at a jog. Then he went back inside, closing and securing the inner door.

Yes, a can of air freshener would be wonderful.

Sally Clarkson sat at her desk, hands shaking with anger. How could he be so rude? She had gone to Andrew Harvey armed with vital information, and he had treated her like ... like the junior analyst she was. Still, he could have at least listened to what she had to say.

After following the trail from Heathrow to Kilburn Park, she had brought up the CCTV archive and watched Rahman Jamshed walk towards the station entrance. He had stopped outside the telephone box and put his hand in his pocket, as if searching for loose change, but once the taxi had moved off, he had walked to the junction and turned right into Alpha Place. Once he had turned the corner, he was out of CCTV coverage, and two hours of scanning the local streets had produced no results.

This was someone who didn't want to be followed, that was for sure. The question was, what was he up to, if anything? That was the question she had wanted to ask Harvey, but he had been unwilling to listen to her. She felt a wave of self-pity wash over her but knew that she couldn't give in to that emotion, so she mumbled, 'Bollocks to you, Andrew Harvey,' and got down to work.

She brought up the file on Abdul Mansour/Ahmed Al-Ali and looked through his history prior to leaving for Pakistan in 2007. There was a list of known associates, and after cross-referencing them, she found only two who still lived within three miles of Kilburn Park station. Jotting down their details, she looked for further links with the area, but the only one she could establish was the mosque near Willesden, about two miles from the station as the crow flies. It had once ranked quite highly on the watch list, but its status had been downgraded in the last year.

Armed with the three addresses, she left the office and went to seek authorisation to perform surveillance under the Regulation of Investigatory Powers Act (RIPA). After explaining the reason for the surveillance, she was given permission and went to the car park to collect her Fiat Punto. Throwing her handbag into the passenger seat, she put the key in the ignition and turned it.

Nothing.

Damn! Not today!

Her battery had been losing its charge overnight for the last week, and she had an appointment with her local garage at the weekend, but that didn't help her at this particular moment, so she went to the back of the car and retrieved the jump pack, a small portable battery designed to provide a jump start when there was no vehicle and set of jump leads available.

She connected the jump pack, climbed in and turned the key. The engine caught at the second attempt, and she removed the connections before returning the pack to the boot.

As she drove north, she formulated her plan. With it being a working day, she didn't expect much response from the residential addresses, and besides, with its previous history she expected the mosque would be more likely to produce results. If she got no result there, she would park up close to one of the private dwellings and observe any comings and goings.

It took nearly an hour to reach her destination, road works and a minor shunt hampering her progress. As she drove past the target building, she was expecting golden minarets or a dome at the very least, but all she saw was a red brick building that could easily have been the headquarters of a small insurance company rather than a place of worship. She drove on until she found a side street to turn around in, then drove back and parked fifty yards from the entrance.

Her watch told her it was just after two in the afternoon. She had no idea what time prayers took place, so she looked up the details on her smart phone. According to the first website she found, it would be within the hour, so she opened the window a fraction to let in a breeze and sat back in her seat to wait it out.

The mosque was in a largely residential area with a few shops at the end of the street, and as a consequence footfall was light. A few mothers passed by, children in tow or riding their pushchairs, but generally the street was quiet for the first half an hour. She checked her reflection in the mirror and once again told herself it was time to lose a few pounds. Her face was growing increasingly rotund, and her short hair did nothing to hide the fact. If she didn't do something about it while she was in her early twenties it would get much harder as the years passed.

As the time approached the top of the hour, people began making their way into the mosque. Most arrived on foot, but it was the party of four that pulled up in a battered Nissan that caught her eye. As the front passenger climbed out, there was something very familiar about him. She couldn't tell if she had been drawn to the large nose or if she had seen him somewhere before. Still racking her brains, she grabbed her smart phone and took a quick photo. Almost as an afterthought, she took pictures of the others exiting the car and then prepared an email before sending it to a colleague back in the office.

As more visitors arrived, she decided to take snaps of as many as she could. Those walking away from her towards the entrance offered no clear shot, but some stopped outside to chat with friends, affording her some decent pictures. She had around twenty images by the time the reply came back from the office, and her heart skipped a beat as she read it.

The man with the large nose was Sami Hussain, and the reason he had looked familiar was that he was a known acquaintance of Ahmed Al-Ali. She had not taken much notice of his profile in her earlier search once she saw he now lived in Coventry, over ninety miles from the mosque. Although there was no law against making such a long journey to attend prayers, the fact that his travelling companions lived even farther north, one in Derby and the other two in Chesterfield, suggested something was brewing, especially as two of them were on the watch list.

Sally opened the window a little more and fished in her bag for the cigarettes, lighting one with a slightly shaking hand. Her nicotine craving satisfied, she prepared another email and attached the other images she had taken. The street was quieter now that prayers had begun, and she took the opportunity to get out and stretch her legs. After crossing the road, she strolled past the entrance to the mosque, throwing a casual glance through the glass pane in the door. As she did, one of the two men standing inside saw the movement from the corner of his eye and watched as she continued past and out of view.

She wasn't sure if she had been noticed until she heard the door open behind her. Were they following her? She wasn't sure and certainly wasn't going to turn around to find out, so she casually continued on to the end of the street and walked into a convenience store, where she purchased more cigarettes. As she came out holding the unopened pack, she saw no sign of anyone suspicious, so she crossed the street and returned to her car, all the time making a conscious effort not to look at the mosque.

As she climbed back inside the car, her phone beeped and she checked the message. Her colleague had run the images through the database and had identified three more people who were on the watch list. One of them lived in London, but the other two had travelled a considerable distance from the southwest coast, and the message told her to report in and await further instructions.

Sally was preparing the report when a yellow coach pulled up outside the mosque, and around thirty men abruptly left the building and climbed aboard. As they filed out, she caught sight of Rahman Jamshed marshalling the men onto the coach, and she added this to the message. There were more details she wanted to add, but the last person climbed on and the coach pulled away, driving past her. She put the phone on the passenger seat, put her seat belt on and turned the ignition, but the engine simply stuttered.

'*No!*' she screamed. She tried again, and after coughing and spluttering, as the battery offered the last ounce of its charge, the engine finally caught. She saw the coach disappearing in her side mirror and did a three-point turn in order to catch up. As she followed it through traffic, she managed to add more details to her report each time they stopped at traffic lights. As they crossed the Thames, she sent the message, including their current heading and the licence number and description of the coach.

They continued south for another ten miles before heading east, with Sally maintaining her observations from three cars behind. Signs for Biggin Hill Airport came and went, and she found herself on the M25, where she let the coach pull ahead, confident of keeping an eye on it. At Junction Five, the coach pulled off onto the Sevenoaks Bypass, and Sally pulled a little closer while still allowing two cars to be between her car and the target vehicle. After another three miles, the coach suddenly pulled into a lay-by, and she was forced to either pull in, too, or carry on and wait for them to catch up. When they moved off, they would have to continue down the same road, so she decided to carry on. At the next junction, she drove round the roundabout until she could see the dual carriageway from the overhead island, and she parked on the grass verge so that she could spot them when they passed.

Keeping one eye on the approaching traffic, she called the office to update her colleague.

Chapter Fifteen

Malik Zarifa walked down the aisle of the coach and stood over Abdul Mansour's seat.

'Brother, we are being followed, just as you predicted. It is the woman I saw at the mosque.'

'Are you sure it is her?' Mansour asked.

'I am certain. As we left, I saw her parked nearby, and the same blue Fiat has been behind us since.'

'Are there any other vehicles following?'

'I have seen none.'

'Okay, thank you, Malik.' Mansour got up and spoke to the driver, instructing him to pull into the lay-by that was coming up. When they parked up, he watched the Fiat continue past and told the driver to open the door. He climbed out and strode to the Nissan waiting for him, and the driver wound down the window.

'We are being followed by a blue Fiat,' Mansour told the driver. 'Drive ahead and check the next junction to see if it is waiting for us.'

The Nissan pulled off, and Mansour pondered the situation. If it were just this woman following, she would be waiting ahead for them to pass by. If there were others following, she would be called off and another car would take her place.

The Nissan returned twenty minutes later, having driven to the next junction, then back to the previous junction, before completing the circuit back to its starting point.

'The car is waiting at the overpass,' the driver told him. 'There is a single passenger, a woman.'

'Very well. When the coach sets off, wait three minutes and then follow it. The driver will lead her to a secluded area, and I want her captured alive. We need to know what she knows.'

The driver nodded and Mansour walked back to the coach, checking his watch. He climbed aboard and told everyone to disembark, and as they did, he gave instructions to the driver. When the last person climbed off, the coach driver set off, and Mansour and his men only had to wait a couple of minutes before the other bus arrived. As they boarded, Mansour watched the Nissan set off, and they followed a minute later, turning off the dual carriageway at the next junction.

Sally's instructions had been specific: If they move off, follow them and give a running commentary until other units could join her; if they don't move off, sit tight. For a long time she thought it would be the latter, but suddenly the coach came into view. She made sure it had the same registration number before rejoining the dual carriageway and tucking in four cars behind it. For four miles they continued south, and then she followed the coach onto a B road. Traffic quickly thinned, and she found herself directly behind the coach, so she dropped her speed to let it pull ahead a little. The scenery became increasingly rural, the road twisting and winding through the countryside, but she was able to see the top of the large coach above the hedges and allowed herself to drop even farther back.

Grabbing the phone from the passenger seat, she hit the speed dial and spoke to her colleague. 'We're on the B2017, heading towards Five Oak Green,' she said.

'Hang on,' she was told, and a moment later the team leader was on the line.

'Sally, good work so far. I want you to hang back and take no chances. We have two ground units en route, and they should be with you within the hour. The chopper had a maintenance issue, but it's on its way now.'

'Will do,' she said, but as she spoke, the coach pulled up a couple of hundred yards ahead. 'Wait, they've stopped.'

'Hold your position,' the team leader told her.

The road was extremely narrow, and she pulled as far onto the grass as she could, but half of the Punto remained on the road. 'Now what?' she asked.

'Hold there, we will have air coverage in fifteen minutes.'

'Okay,' she said, and ended the call. A yellow light on the dashboard grabbed her attention: the fuel reserve warning.

'Shit.' She had filled the car up only two weeks previously. But then she realised the driving she had done today was not part of her normal daily routine, and that would have taken its toll. Her back-up would arrive within the hour, but what if the coach set off before they arrived? Even if it stayed still, she still had to drive home and hadn't noticed a petrol station on her journey down. With no choice but to reserve her fuel, she turned the ignition off and sat in silence.

For a few minutes there was no movement, no sound except the occasional bird call. As she kept an eye on the coach in the distance, she saw the red car approaching in her door mirror. She was confident that she had left enough room for it to pass, so she was seriously pissed when it crawled by and took her door mirror off. The car parked up just in front of hers, and the driver got out, surveying the damage he had caused. As he did, Sally saw the glint of metal in his waistband.

All thoughts now turned to self-preservation. Her hand shot to the ignition, and for the final time her car let her down. The man was already at her door, tugging at the handle, but her habit was to lock the door every time she got in, the result of a friend having been carjacked the previous year.

She grabbed the phone, but before she could hit the speed dial, a bullet shattered the side window, the round flashing by her right ear and burying itself in the passenger door. Sally let out a scream and covered her ears, the sound of the blast still resonating.

The gunman unlocked the door through the broken window and opened it, grabbing her by the hair and sticking the barrel of the gun into her temple.

'Out,' he ordered, and Sally shakily complied, tears now running down her cheeks.

The gunman reached into her car and grabbed the phone and her handbag, before dragging her towards the Nissan, the rear door already opened from the inside by a passenger. The gunman pushed her inside, and the passenger dragged her the rest of the way in before placing a hood over her head and pushing her to the floor well.

The driver got back in, and they sped off towards the coach. When they reached it, he beeped his horn and the coach driver emerged, gave them a wave and disappeared back inside, heading for the back seats. After puncturing a can of petrol he splashed the contents over the seats as he made his way towards the entrance. At the door he flicked his Zippo lighter, got a good flame and threw it as far into the interior as he could manage, before running to the open passenger door of the Nissan. He got in and slammed the door, the car speeding away as the first flames began licking the windows of the coach.

The satellite navigation system told Andrew Harvey to turn off the A23 at the next junction and led him towards Tom Gray's location. After popping over to the Home Office building to collect Gray's document, he had driven down the M23, his headache increasing in intensity with every mile. His watch had told him he had over an hour to spare, so he'd pulled in at Pease Pottage services and grabbed a coffee and some max-strength pain-relief tablets. That had been thirty minutes earlier, and he could now feel the headache waning.

When he got to within half a mile of his destination, he came across the first cordon that had been set up, a police car blocking the road and a detour sign pointing towards the country lane on his right. His eyes followed the arrow, and he saw that several news agencies had sent outside broadcasting units, their vans lining the side of the road as far as the eye could see, cameras pointing at Gray's building in the hope of catching any unfolding drama.

Harvey pulled up and waited for the officer to approach, before flashing his identity card and explaining the purpose of his visit. The officer had to call his superiors to get clarification, but after a minute or two the police car was moved aside, and he was waved through. Beyond the police car was another, its nose pointing towards the entrance to Gray's compound which lay six hundred yards down the road. As he drove down the lane, he saw Gray's building off to the right, all but the roof hidden by the hedges which surrounded the entire compound. When he pulled up at the command centre, he was greeted by Evan Davies.

'Mr Harvey, Major Blythe is expecting you.' He led Harvey into the vehicle where the Major, wearing civvies, stood with a phone in his hand. They waited for him to finish his conversation before Davies made the introductions.

Harvey held up the document he was carrying. 'I have to go and give it to him,' he said.

Blythe nodded. 'While you're there, I need you to gather as much information as you can,' he said. 'We haven't been able to get very close, so I need to know what defences he has on that path, if any. I also want you to try and get inside, let us know about any weapons he has, the layout, where the prisoners are being held, where he sits, what equipment he has—everything.'

'I hear he released one of the boys,' Harvey said. 'Where is he?'

'He was taken to hospital. He seemed healthy enough, apart from the smashed hands. I think it was Gray's way of making sure he didn't go straight back to burglary.'

'Didn't you manage to get anything out of him before he left?'

'Nothing,' Blythe said. 'He was in his cell all day, and all he could hear was mumblings from the other hostages. He couldn't even hear Gray when his cell door was closed, which was most of the time.'

'He must have seen something when he walked out.'

Blythe shook his head. 'Gray put a hood over his head before he released him, and he didn't walk out. He'd been sitting on a box for the last four days and couldn't stand up, so Gray dragged him out by his hands, and as he'd just had them crushed, you can understand that he was a bit more focused on the pain than his surroundings.'

Harvey could indeed imagine the pain he was in, having broken a wrist in a motorcycle accident while on holiday the previous year. 'I'll get all the information I can,' he said. He pulled out his mobile phone and called Gray.

'I'm here, Tom.'

'Have you got the agreement?' Gray asked.

'Right here. Want me to bring it in?'

'Sure, come on over. Don't hang up; just walk nice and slowly up to the front door.'

Harvey nodded to Blythe and left the vehicle. Turning left into the compound, he strolled up to the front of the building. When he was twenty yards from the main door, Gray told him to stop. 'Put the phone and agreement on the ground and remove your jacket.'

Harvey did as he was told, then picked up the phone. 'Turn round slowly and raise your shirt.' Again Harvey complied. After following further instructions to raise his trouser legs to reveal his ankles, he was told to approach the door. He did so slowly, trying to identify any dangers on the path or off to the side. He saw nothing. There were mounds in the dirt either side of the path, but he recognised the three-pronged triggers sticking out of them as belonging to anti-personnel mines rather than claymores. These mines would only go off if someone stood on them, whereas claymores could be detonated remotely.

The door opened as he got to it, and before him stood Tom Gray, one hand out ready to accept the agreement, the other clutching the trigger to the grenades on his waistcoat. Harvey kept the document by his side. 'Aren't you going to invite me in?' he asked, manoeuvring his body to get a better view inside the building.

'Nice try, Andrew, but I'm not about to compromise my combat effectiveness by letting you know what I have in here.' He clicked his fingers and gestured towards the agreement again. Harvey handed it over, and Gray made to close the door.

'Wait,' Harvey said. Gray paused to listen, face impassive. 'Why did you do that to Harper? I thought we had a deal, and the public certainly didn't vote for that.'

Gray shrugged. 'If he had lasted to the end of the week, he would have been birched—which would have been a deterrent— or killed. As he left early, that was my reminder that he should change his ways. He won't be in a position to break the law for a while, and that means he will have time to reflect.'

'The home secretary won't be pleased,' Harvey told him.

'Perhaps. But everyone living near Adrian Harper will be a lot safer for the next few months, and that's who I care about, not some bloated politician who takes credit for others' work.'

Gray went to close the door, and Harvey took a step forward, sticking his foot in the gap. 'Why did you ask me to come down here? Why not someone else?'

Gray pushed the door open and threw Harvey a look which told him to move back quickly or suffer the consequences. Harvey took the hint, retreating a couple of steps.

'I wanted to see who I was up against,' Gray said. 'There's only so much you can find out about a person over the phone. Looking a man in the eye, seeing the way he carries himself, you can learn a lot about an adversary.'

'And what, exactly, have you learnt?'

'Well, your appearance suggests that you pay attention to detail, you obviously keep fit, and you seem calm under pressure. That tells me that you shouldn't be underestimated.'

Harvey's expression didn't change; he just stared at Gray, taking his own chance to weigh him up.

'See you soon,' Gray said, and closed the door.

Harvey walked back to the command vehicle, collecting his jacket on the way. Blythe was waiting for him and wasn't impressed that he was back so soon.

'Well, that taught us a lot,' he said, disappointment etched all over his face.

'If that had been you in there, would you have let me in?' Harvey asked, not even waiting for a reply. 'He knows why I wanted to look around inside because he isn't as stupid as you might think he is. You should bear that in mind, because if you underestimate him, it could cost lives.'

'I don't underestimate him by any stretch of the imagination. I know his reputation within the Regiment, and he is highly regard- ed. I'm just frustrated that we can't seem to gain any advantage. Did you learn anything there?'

'I couldn't see inside. Behind him, all I could see was a wall. I don't know if you go through the door and turn left or turn right, so you would have to split your forces straight away.

'Outside, all I saw were anti-personnel mines, nothing that could be detonated remotely.'

'He has had plenty of time to adapt them for remote detonation,' Blythe reminded him.

'True, but the triggers are level with the ground. If they were to inflict damage to anyone on the path, they would be angled towards it.'

Blythe noted the clever observation, regretting having been so short with him earlier, but before he could comment, Harvey took his leave and began the journey north, hoping the rush-hour traffic would allow him to be back in the office in time to see the result of the voting.

As he made his way up the M23, he thought about what Gray had said, that looking a man in the eye told you something about him. He had to concede that there was some truth in it, because having met Gray, he now realised how focused he was. There was no sign of anxiety that would have marked him as unpredictable. Gray was a man in control of his destiny. It was then that Harvey realised the true purpose of the meeting: it hadn't been so that Gray could weigh up Harvey; it was the other way round.

Chapter Sixteen

As the coach pulled up to the barn, the door was opened by the farmer, and the driver pulled up inside. Abdul Mansour was the first off, and the rest of the passengers followed, taking in their new surroundings as the barn door closed to hide them from prying eyes. One side of the barn was stacked to the roof with hay, the other side with straw, and at the far end there was a pile of logs cut into eight-inch lengths. The wood was stacked three feet high and protruded from the wall by a yard and a half.

The farmer introduced himself as Flynn—Mansour didn't know if it was his first name or surname, nor did he care—and pointed to the logs. 'Let's shift this lot,' he said to Mansour, who struggled to understand his heavy Irish accent.

He had been reluctant to use the IRA after they had double-crossed the Syrians back in the eighties, but his masters had insisted that they were the only option, with time against them, so messages had been exchanged, and two million dollars had been transferred to their account. Despite his misgivings, Mansour wasn't about to do anything to jeopardise his rise to greatness, which so far had been meteoric.

Ahmed Al-Ali had always been a devout follower of Islam and had attended the mosque near Kilburn since his parents moved to the area when he was just nine years old. The next few years had been distinctly uneventful, with nothing more interesting than a couple of fistfights to break up the cycle of school, prayers, home-work and sleep, until the death of the imam just after his sixteenth birthday.

The old man had been loved and respected by the community, and his passing had saddened them all. Hundreds attended the funeral to pay their respects, and afterwards the topic of conversation had turned to who his successor was going to be.

The answer had come just a few days later in the form of Amir Channa. His initial teachings followed on from those of the previous imam, but there had been a gradual introduction of political themes, subtly at first to allow him to gauge the reaction, becoming more intense as time went on.

As Ahmed was approaching his seventeenth birthday, the imam had asked him to attend a protest organised by the Stop the War Coalition, and that was when he had been introduced to Nazeem. He hadn't offered a surname, and Ahmed had never asked: he suspected Nazeem wasn't even his real first name.

Where Channa was the prospector, tasked only with finding the rough diamonds, Nazeem was the jeweller who shaped them into something beautiful. He took Ahmed under his wing and fed him stories from back home, of the struggle against the infidels, the oppression of the faithful in their own land.

Ahmed had been a willing apprentice and quick to learn, and after three short months he had made such progress that he'd been offered the chance to go to the homeland and make a proper contribution to the fight.

'I want you to think about it carefully,' Nazeem had said. 'It will mean saying goodbye to your family forever.'

Ahmed had agreed without hesitation. He was an only child, and his father had ensured a strict upbringing. There had been no love, only beatings when he showed any disobedience. From the age of three he had been given chores to do, and there was a leather strap waiting if they weren't done properly and in time. There was always a surreptitious hug from his mother afterwards, her semi-sweet voice begging him to obey his father, before giving him more chores to complete.

And so, with less than a hundred pounds in his pocket and a few changes of clothes in his bag, Ahmed Al-Ali had taken the Pakistan International Airways flight to Quetta, changing planes in Lahore. He had been met at the airport, driven the six miles to the capital of the Balochistan province and dropped at a house which was nothing more than a shack made from corrugated iron. He'd been fed and given a bed for the night, and before dawn he was awoken by yet more strangers and driven out of civilisation and into the wilderness.

The journey took him past mountains and over the border into Afghanistan. Their vehicle turned off the main road onto a dirt track, which ended hours later at the base of a mountain range. For another four hours he had been guided at an unrelenting pace through the hills by a man who hadn't spoken more than a handful of words all day. After being handed off to another guide waiting in the hills, he'd arrived at the camp an hour later.

At first he had been treated like any other recruit, sharing a tent with seven others and helping with the cooking and guard duty. However, he took to the AK-47 like he had been born with one, able to hit a target the size of a human head from four hundred yards, considered the maximum effective range of the weapon. He'd also showed an aptitude for explosives, able to create an improvised explosive device within ten minutes.

When an American patrol had been ambushed and captured, they had been taken to the camp, and Ahmed was given his first major test by the mullahs. They asked him to dispatch one of the three captives and handed him the Marine's handgun, but instead he had taken out his knife and slit the soldier's throat, maintaining eye contact until the man took his last breath. That demonstration of ruthlessness elevated him in their eyes, and he was no longer considered the coddled outsider.

From that moment on Ahmed had adopted the name Abdul Mansour, casting off the final tie to his previous life. The name meant 'servant of God and is victorious', which he thought an apt description.

The first sortie he took part in had not gone well, with sixteen of the twenty men in the team being killed while attacking a supply convoy. Air support had been called in and the Apache helicopters had decimated them, but Abdul had completed his part of the mission, destroying the fuel tanker before leading the survivors to safety.

With so many men lost, Abdul had been promoted and given a team of his own, which he led to many successes due to his astute tactics, tactics which had impressed the mullahs so much that he was involved in all further planning.

It was Abdul Mansour who had seen the beginnings of the Tom Gray saga and had come up with the plan to deal a blow to the infidels on their own soil, and after listening to his idea, they had immediately put things into motion.

Now here he was, less than ten miles from his target and about to share the plan with his men. First, though, he had to ensure that the weapons they were going to use were fit for purpose, so he instructed his men to move the logs as the Irishman had ordered.

With the wood gone, Mansour saw a trapdoor with a rusty ring as a handle. Two men lifted the door, and the Irishman went down the stairs, followed closely by Mansour. Shelves ran down the sides of the cellar, three on each side and all filled with wooden boxes. Flynn gestured to Mansour to give him a hand, and they lifted a box off a shelf and placed it on the floor. Using a crowbar, the Irishman took the lid off to reveal a dozen AK-47s wrapped in wax paper. Mansour took one out and examined it, checking the mechanism before deftly stripping it down and inspecting the barrel. The rifle had been well looked after, and he nodded his head.

'What about the rest?'

Flynn pointed to five other boxes. 'The rest of the AK-47s, ammunition, the grenades and the C4.'

'I'll need a pistol.'

'That wasn't on the list,' Flynn said, sounding like a dodgy plumber, 'but I'll throw in a Browning.'

Mansour feigned appreciation. 'Thanks. And the rocket-propelled grenades?'

The Irishman led him to the back of the cellar, where a long box lay on the floor, supported by two-inch blocks of wood to protect it from damp.

'Four RPGs, as requested.'

Mansour opened the box and pulled out an RPG-22 he had become familiar with back home.

'These are single-shot weapons. We requested RPG-7s.'

'This is all we got,' Flynn said with a shrug.

'Then we will need twice as many.'

'As I said, this is all we got.'

Mansour cursed inwardly, his reticence in using these people fully justified. Still, it was too late to do anything about it now: their time would come. He shouted to his men to come down and get the boxes.

'I'll need lots of cleaning kits,' he told Flynn, who pointed at a cardboard box on a shelf. Mansour carried it upstairs and got the more experienced men to supervise the weapon stripping and cleaning, helping those who had never seen an AK-47 before. While they did this, Mansour asked Flynn to show him the getaway vehicles.

The Irishman took him around the back of the barn where seven cars were parked. All were saloons around three years old and in good condition.

'Where did you get them?' Mansour asked.

'All stolen in the last couple of days and fitted with plates that relate to similar vehicles, so you shouldn't get stopped by the police ANPR units.' The automatic number plate recognition system was the bane of the illegal driver; it was able to read a number plate and run it against information gained from several agencies, letting the police officers know within a couple of seconds if it was stolen or the driver had no insurance.

Flynn headed for the farmhouse and Mansour returned to the barn, telling his twenty-seven men to gather round so that he could explain their mission.

'Brothers, we have been given a unique opportunity to hit the infidels on their own soil, and we must strike in the next twenty-four hours. The beautiful irony is that the hard work has already been done by one of their own.'

He looked at the men to see if anyone understood what he had in mind, but all he saw were blank faces, so he laid out the plan in simple terms.

'You have all seen the news story about Tom Gray, have you not?'

Nods all round.

'Then you know that he has planted a device somewhere in this country, a device that he claims will kill many people.'

'Are we going to look for his bomb?' one asked.

'That won't be easy,' another pointed out. 'If the police can't find it, how do we get our hands on it?'

Willing, they certainly were; intelligent, they were not. 'We do not need to find the device. We simply need to prevent Tom Gray from giving away its location.' He let the words sink in, eventually seeing realisation dawn. 'We expected to have until Thursday to complete our mission, but news of this agreement has brought the deadline forward. We must strike tomorrow, and strike hard. Once Gray is dead, the country will panic. No one will go near a city centre on Friday, and that will hit the economy hard. There won't be thousands of deaths as Gray predicted, but it will strike fear in the hearts of the people, and their anger will be directed at their government for failing to protect them.'

He studied the men, his voice conveying the solemnity of their mission.

'What we do tomorrow, we do for Allah. He has given us the courage in our hearts to complete this deed, and we do so in His name. Not all of us will survive the next twenty-four hours, and those that make the sacrifice will have their reward in *Jannah*, the Garden of Heaven. Those that do make it will live to do Allah's work another day.'

He was pleased that none of the faces showed any signs of unease.

'We are not facing one man. He is surrounded by police,' one said. 'How are we going to get to him?'

'Yes, we need to know what we are facing. How many people are protecting him?' another asked.

Mansour was glad that some were already thinking tactically. 'The police are there to keep civilians and the media out of harm's way, not to protect him. Our attack will be the last thing they expect.'

'Are they armed?'

'How many are there?'

The questions came thick and fast, so Mansour held up his hands for silence. 'I will explain the plan and take your questions later.

'Firstly, the British media have given us all of the information we need. They have shown the number of police surrounding the area, and from those pictures we know that they are carrying arms. Those men are SO15, their Counter Terrorism Command, and they know how to shoot. However, it is easy for us to get within two hundred yards of them and still find cover.'

He knelt down and drew a square on the dirt floor with his finger. 'There are hedges running down two sides of his compound, here on the left and to the south. To the right the land rises away from his building and then slopes down, forming a ridge. This gives us the high ground.

'Along the south side of the compound, there are several media vehicles, and in the bottom left hand corner, here, there are two police vehicles. There are men stationed around the building, thirty yards apart, forming a semicircle from here to here, covering the south and east. Finally, in the top left-hand corner we have the command vehicles.

'We will approach from the east, and two cars will park at the head of the media vans, here. In these cars will be the six men who will take up their position on the ridge. The rest of the cars will carry on, one parking at the other end of the line of media vans, the rest parking near the two police vehicles here.

'I will be in the last car to arrive and will be carrying two of the RPGs, which I will use to take out the police cars. Everyone else in these four cars will follow up and kill any survivors and then split up, ten going for the command vehicles, the rest towards the media vans.'

'Do we kill the reporters?'

'Not unless you have to. I will assign four people to round them up and put them in one vehicle while the rest fire at the police in the field from behind the hedge. We will use the reporters as a shield, which should limit the amount of return fire.

'Once the first shot is fired, the first six men we dropped off will move to the ridge and lay down fire. Of the ten men heading for the command vehicles, four will position themselves along the hedge here and keep the police in the compound pinned down, while the remaining six will attack the vehicles themselves.

'I need two volunteers who are able to ride these motorcycles,' he said, pointing to a couple of dirt bikes leaning against bales of straw. 'You must be able to ride off-road at high speed.' Several hands went up. 'Okay, you will all have a go later, and I will pick the best two.'

He grabbed an RPG and held it up. 'Who has fired one of these before?'

Only one hand went up this time. 'Okay, Zulfir, you will be in the team on the ridge. That gives you a clean shot at his front door, and we are counting on you to provide a way in. On my signal you will take the doors out and everyone will move in. Fire and move, fire and move. Half of you will provide covering fire, while the other half move ten yards closer to the building. The rest will then move ten yards past your position and cover you while you do the same. You keep doing this until you have cleared a path for the men on the bikes. They will approach from over the ridge and ride to the door, dismount and run inside.

'Once Gray is dead, you all return to your vehicles and disperse. Make sure that when you exit your vehicles, you leave the engines running.'

Mansour looked around at the men before him. Some were older than his twenty-one years, the majority younger, but all looked pumped up, eager to get going. It was time to bring them back to reality.

'After we have finished preparing the weapons, I will assign your positions, and then we will practise our attack, again and again, until you all know your responsibilities. Finally, we will pray to Allah and thank Him for this opportunity.'

At that moment the barn door opened a crack, and Flynn squeezed through the gap. 'Someone's coming,' he said.

Mansour went to the door and saw the red Nissan approaching. 'It's okay, they're with us.'

The Irishman opened the door fully to allow the car in and closed it behind them. The driver got out and pulled a sobbing Sally from the back seat, the hood still in place.

Mansour looked at her hands and legs, which were shaking like leaves in a hurricane. This woman was scared, well outside of her comfort zone. She should be easy to crack.

'Take her to the cellar,' he said in his native tongue. 'Tie her hands and legs, and keep a guard on her. I will deal with her later.'

As Sally was taken away, Mansour called Zulfir over.

'You are the only one who knows how to fire the RPG, but I don't like to put all of my eggs in one basket. I will assign five others to be with you on the ridge, and you must show them all how to fire the weapon, just in case anything happens to you.'

Zulfir nodded, not even slightly offended by the suggestion that he might not be able to complete the job. 'Yes, brother.'

Chapter Seventeen

Andrew Harvey was halfway back to London when he got the call, and he activated his hands-free set.

'Harvey.'

'Andrew, what's your position?' Hammond asked.

'I'm on the M23, about seven miles south of the M25.'

'You need to turn around. We have a situation. Punch this location into your satnav.'

Hammond gave him the postcode, and Harvey saw that it was close by. 'What's the problem?'

'One of our analysts, Sally Clarkson, was tailing suspects when she went off grid.'

Harvey's heart missed a beat at the sound of her name. A couple of times during the day, he had thought about the way he had dismissed her, deciding an apology was definitely in order. Now she appeared to be in dire trouble, and it was all his fault.

'I gave her that assignment,' he said. 'I thought it was a false alarm, given Mansour's status, but she obviously found something. Do you have any details?'

'Looks like Rahman Jamshed turned out to be Abdul Mansour after all. She found him at a mosque in Willesden, where he boarded a bus with about thirty others, a few of which are on our watch list. She tailed them to her current location, but by the time help arrived she was gone and the coach was in flames.'

'They must have transferred to another coach; they can't all be on foot. Can we get a chopper up to search the area?'

'Already there, but there were just a few cars in the area, nothing that could hold thirty people, and thermal images showed no one hiding in the nearby fields.'

'Okay, I'm on my way. Send me everything she reported in.'

The satnav told him to leave the motorway at junction nine, then led him through B roads for forty minutes until he came across the fire engines. Two surveillance units were already on hand and a scene of crime officer was dusting the Fiat's door for fingerprints. Harvey approached the SOCO first.

'Got anything yet?' he asked, flashing his ID.

The SOCO looked at the card, shook his head and returned to his work, so Harvey went to speak to his colleagues.

'What do we know so far?'

'We know Sally has been taken at gunpoint,' John Collins told him. He began giving a rundown of the events, but Harvey stopped him.

'I listened to the recordings on the way down. I know she got to here; now we need to know where she went. What's the story with the coach?'

'Booked yesterday from Duckitt Travel and paid cash when they picked it up this morning,' Collins said. 'The owners weren't happy when they heard what happened to it.'

'I'll bet. So who rented it?'

'Mohammed Ali. That's the Muslim equivalent of John Smith.'

Harvey stared at the coach, the flames now extinguished and the firemen going through the damping-down process. 'There were thirty men on that coach, and they've disappeared. They must have transferred to another vehicle, be it another coach, or three minibuses or seven cars. Have you checked other hire companies?'

Billy Emerson shook his head, and Harvey called Farsi, throwing his colleagues an admonishing look. 'Hamad, we need to find any coaches rented today. Look for anything booked yesterday, particularly anything booked by a Mohammed Ali and paid in cash. We know he booked one with Duckitt Travel. We need to see if he booked any others elsewhere. It might by a single coach or multiple minibuses. Whichever it is, it will probably be self-drive.

'Can you also send me Mansour's file? I read the summary, but I need to know all I can about this guy.'

He pocketed the phone and started to say something to Emerson, but caught himself in time. It wasn't up to these guys to investigate all the possibilities; it was his, and the last thing he needed to do was alienate anyone else. 'I think they came down here and noticed they were being followed, so they stopped, picked her up and carried on. That means they were heading south, which is where we need to concentrate our search.'

He strode over to the burnt-out coach and eventually found the sub officer. 'Can you tell us anything?' he asked.

'Nothing much at the moment. An accelerant was used, probably petrol, but you'll be hard pressed to get any prints or DNA. This was an old coach—lots of combustible material used in its construction. That's why it went up so quick.'

As he spoke, the roof at the rear of the coach collapsed, debris falling into the interior. Harvey thanked him and returned to the surveillance team. 'There's nothing for us here, and I'm starving. Let's head south, find a café and grab a bite. I think it's going to be a long night.'

Chapter Eighteen

Abdul Mansour took the men with weapons experience aside and gave them their instructions.

'Take them into the field and run them through the drill. Show them how to hold a rifle, how to aim, how to squeeze the trigger rather than pull it, how to change the magazine, how to clear a blockage—everything. They need a three-month course in the next three hours.'

He stared into the field, imagining the scene they would face.

'Give them some targets to aim at. Policemen, Gray's building, police cars—everything.'

The seven men nodded in unison, ideas forming in their minds.

'Start them all off as if they were getting out of their vehicles, and give them their positions. Do you remember the instructions I gave?'

More nods.

'Okay. There are thirty-one of us, including myself. Three of you will go right, taking nine men towards the media vans. Two of you will take another eight towards the command vehicle. There will be two on the bikes, and the remaining two of you will be among the six on the ridge. I will take an observation role near the coach. When the path is cleared for the bikes, I will blow a whistle twice, two long blasts. When it is time to retreat, I will blow multiple short blasts.

'Any questions?'

There were none.

'Good. Mahmood, I want you to take the ones who can ride a bike, and see what they can do. Find me two who can cover two hundred yards in the quickest time.'

Mahmood nodded and Mansour left them to their duties, heading off to speak to his hostage. As he entered the barn, he saw the two guards playing around, laughing and aiming at each other with their new weapons. He strode over and delivered a punch to the head of the larger member of the duo, sending him sprawling. The man lay on the ground, massaging his jaw, staring at him with incomprehension.

'Who is looking after the girl?' Mansour roared.

'The Irishman said he would watch over her,' the other guard said meekly.

'And what do you know about this man? Would you trust him with your life?'

The guard shook his head. 'No, brother.'

'This isn't a holiday, Sami. This is war. If I give you instructions, you follow them or people die.'

'I'm sorry, brother.'

Mansour grabbed Sami's gun and checked the chamber before showing it to the guard. 'You were pointing a loaded weapon at one of your own men. How many times have you used one of these?'

'Never, brother. I was given it just now.'

Mansour was furious. Under different circumstances he would have taken them aside and shown them the error of their ways with a bullet to the head, but he needed every available man for the mission ahead. Instead, he removed the magazine and ejected the round from the chamber, before handing the weapon back.

'Get everyone outside. The training begins now.'

As the men filed outside, he went down into the cellar, where he found Flynn with his hand inside the hostage's blouse. The Irishman, so immersed in the moment, didn't hear him arrive.

'Do you mind if I speak to my prisoner?' Mansour asked.

Flynn jumped, embarrassment etched on his face, but he soon regained his composure. 'Just getting to know her,' he said, a smile forming.

'Don't bother. She won't be around for long.'

Flynn looked at the woman, admiring the body. Maybe carrying a couple of pounds too many, but still attractive. 'Now that would be a waste,' he said. 'Why not leave her to me when you've finished? You're a guest here, and it's always wise to keep your host happy. Besides, we can call it payment for the Browning.'

Mansour considered the statement and recognised the veiled threat. There was no telling what this snake would do if he refused his request, and he couldn't afford any complications at this late stage.

'Fine. Once I have finished with her, she is all yours.'

Flynn patted him on the shoulder on his way out of the cellar. 'Be gentle with her. I don't like damaged goods.'

Mansour bit his lip. The insolence of this man knew no bounds! He forced the thought from his mind and concentrated on the woman. She still wore the hood, so he had no idea what she looked like. Her bag was on the cellar floor, so he picked it up, looking for some form of identification. He found the two images of him, one taken during his days as Ahmed Al-Ali; the most recent, taken at the airport. He also found her wallet, and an ID badge said her name was Sarah Clark.

I don't think so, he thought to himself. The UK Border Agency weren't known for covert surveillance, which meant this badge was a forgery, and only the Security Service would be able to create something like this.

He studied the picture, and the face staring back was rather plain. Did the Irishman know what he was going to be getting? Probably not, but then he doubted he cared, the pudgy fifty-year-old lucky to get any kind of female at all.

'What's your real name?' he asked her, but got no reply. She was breathing heavily, her body shaking, possibly because of her pawing by Flynn, most likely because of the situation in general. Mansour wasn't about to put her at ease, preferring to deal with the frightened child inside her. He drew his knife and placed the sharp point of the blade into her throat.

'I asked you a question, and I am not noted for my patience,' he said, pressing the point in a little harder, drawing a drop of blood.

'Sarah Clark,' she whimpered.

Mansour moved the knife down her chest, past her open blouse, and sliced through the front strap of her bra, then moved the material to reveal her right breast. He placed the blade beneath the mound of flesh.

'Try again.'

'Sally!' she screamed. 'Sally Clarkson!'

Mansour kept the knife in place. 'And who do you work for, Sally. If you tell me it's the UK Border Agency, I will slice your breast off.'

'The Security Service,' she cried, bursting into tears.

'MI5? I didn't know they employed anyone so incompetent. What is your role?'

'I'm an ... an analyst.'

'What does that involve?'

'Data mining, looking for trends, things like that,' she said, her voice still trembling.

'So why did they send you to follow me?'

Sally told him the whole story, from Harvey's outburst, right up to the moment of her capture. Mansour believed her and wasn't happy with the confirmation that the intelligence agencies knew of his presence in Britain. They would certainly be looking for him as well as the woman, but the only clue they had was her last location, which was over forty miles away. Still, it didn't do to underestimate the enemy.

The authorities would certainly have aircraft up looking for them, so doing the training out in the open was perhaps not the best idea, but he had to weigh up the risk of detection against the need to familiarise the men with their mission.

He decided to give them forty minutes, then get everyone inside for further weapons training. After ensuring that the woman was securely bound to the wooden chair she was sitting on, he went outside to oversee the training.

As he stood in the centre of the field, watching as his recruits carried out the instructions they had been given, he tried not to allow the frustration to show on his face. This was only their second attempt, but still they faced more of a threat from each other than the police. The field was roughly the same size as Gray's, and bales of straw had been set up to represent the enemy, with a tractor taking on the role of the target building.

It was unfortunate that he couldn't test their proficiency with the weapons, instead having them shout, 'Bang! Bang!' to simulate each round being fired. If he allowed any rounds to go off, the sound would travel, and although they were isolated here, there was always the chance someone would hear the reports.

He shouted for them to stop and the men obeyed, remaining in their current positions. He strode to the group advancing from the ridge—actually a line of straw bales—and pointed out their mistakes. 'You are too close together. You three are supposed to give covering fire while the other three advance, but look at their position now.'

The men looked, but the expressions on their faces told him they saw nothing. 'Your field of fire is too small. You can only point your weapon three inches this way and three inches that way. Any more than that, and you will hit your own men.' He instructed the men to move apart by another ten yards, and the three in the firing positions immediately noticed the difference.

'Syed, Irfan, show me your weapons.'

The men handed over the rifles, and Mansour looked at the fire selector. 'What setting is that?' he asked Syed, handing the weapon back. The recruit checked and confirmed that it was set to fully automatic.

'I want all weapons on semi-automatic tomorrow.' He held up the other weapon in the firing position. 'Breathe, aim, squeeze; breathe, aim, squeeze. Firing single shots will preserve your ammunition and give you greater accuracy. If you just spray the enemy on fully automatic you will exhaust a magazine in seconds and give them the advantage, allowing them to close on your position while you reload.'

He handed the rifle back to Irfan. 'Back to your start positions. Let's do it again.'

This time they did better, but in his heart he knew that there was very little chance of any of them surviving the assault. Allah would receive them and would show His gratitude, and then He would put steel in the hearts of others to take their place.

A drop of rain landed on his face and he stared at the heavens, watching as the grey clouds moved slowly towards them. The weather forecast was for light rain over the next two days, which suited him perfectly. The police protecting Gray would be demoralised, and he would attack with men pumped up for the mission.

He instructed his men to go through it one more time, then return to the barn, while he himself went to see how the five volunteers were getting on with the bikes.

Mahmood pointed out the two most promising riders, and Mansour summoned them over.

'What are your names?' he asked.

'Kamran.'

'Nadeem.'

'I hear you handle those bikes well,' he said to them, and watched the smiles appear on their faces. 'Are you willing to take on the role tomorrow?'

They both nodded, smiles remaining in place.

'And do you believe in your hearts that what we do tomorrow needs to be done?'

'Of course, brother. This is *jihad*.'

Mansour knew they were applying the translation commonly used by western civilisations—'holy war.' In fact, *jihad* meant 'struggle', notably the struggle to defend Islam. Still, if it helped them to complete their mission, it didn't matter how they interpreted it.

'Allah has chosen you for a reason,' he said, and saw their chests puff with pride. 'When you get to the entrance of the building, you will be facing a man with years of combat experience. Neither of you have ever held a weapon, so you would prove no match in a gunfight. That is why I want you each to wear an explosive vest and detonate it once you get inside.'

He didn't quite get the reaction he hoped for, with both of the men losing their smiles, but a moment later first one, then the other, nodded.

'I will do this for Allah,' one said.

'*Allahu Akbar,*' the other proclaimed. Allah is the Greatest.

'*Allahu Akbar,*' Mansour agreed. 'Come. It is time to pray.'

Chapter Nineteen

Tom Gray removed his laptop from the table and placed it on one of the feeding trolleys, then pushed the table into Joseph Olemwu's cell, parking it up against the left-hand wall.

'It's time, Joseph,' he said, removing the tape over his mouth before unlocking the shackles on the boy's ankles. Olemwu waited until both feet were free, then kicked out, catching Gray on the chin with the bridge of his foot. Gray staggered backwards but gathered himself immediately, the boy's weakened leg muscles having failed to deliver a telling blow.

'You really are a dumb fuck,' he said, massaging his jaw. 'You should have at least waited until I untied your hand. Now what are you going to do?'

Olemwu's silence told him he hadn't thought that far ahead. He had tried talking his way to freedom earlier in the day, but once he'd realised that this approach wasn't going to work, he had resorted to the only other thing he knew—violence—and his rational thought process had once again abandoned him.

Gray untied the rope connecting Olemwu's left wrist to the ring on the wall, then grabbed his arm and picked him up, swinging him around so that he was bent double over the table. Once his wrists had been tied to another ring he wrapped his belt around the boy's legs and secured it tightly just above the knees. With the preparations complete, he wheeled the trolley into the cell and focused the laptop's built-in webcam so that it showed Olemwu lying across the table, his toes just about touching the floor and three-day-old faeces crusting the crack of his bare backside.

His watch told him he had a few minutes until the broadcast was due, so he left the cell to escape the smell, closing the door behind him. Olemwu kicked off big time, shouting, swearing and thrashing about, but he ignored the commotion and climbed the stairs to the first floor, stopping at one of the windows. Although it appeared to be completely boarded up from the outside, the bottom panel was hinged, allowing it to be swung upwards. The three-inch gap would allow him to lay down suppressing fire, should the need arise.

He opened the panel and put his face to the gap, breathing deeply. The cool evening air was like nectar, and he drank deeply, savouring the taste of the countryside.

All too soon it was time to speak to the nation again, so he put the panel back in place and made his way downstairs to where Olemwu was still causing a huge fuss. He entered the cell, and Olemwu immediately began pleading with him, begging for mercy.

'Fat chance,' Gray said.

Gray hit the 'Play' button on the laptop's streaming software and took a couple of steps backwards.

'People of Britain, the results of the votes for Joseph Olemwu should be on your screens now. As you can see, only 37 percent of the voters want Joseph to die, the rest wanting to see him birched.

'So be it.'

He disappeared off the screen for a moment and returned with the birch in his hand.

'Normally, I would tell you to send the children out of the room at this point, but if you have kids over twelve years of age, you should let them watch this so that they know what they might face if they decide to break the law.'

Olemwu began pleading again, his voice high-pitched and strained, but Gray ignored him and delivered the first stroke. The boy screamed, and a thick weal immediately appeared on his buttocks. The next blow landed an inch lower.

'*Ow!*'

Tears streamed down Olemwu's face, and he sobbed like a three-year-old, but Gray continued regardless, opening up the first weal with his third stroke. He cursed inwardly because he hadn't intended to draw blood. The purpose of the exercise was to show the effect of the birch as a deterrent, not its ability to wound, and this could turn people against its reintroduction. He gave Olemwu another three strokes, taking care to hit undamaged skin each time, then put the birch down and turned to face the camera.

'As you can see, Joseph—who considers himself a bit of a hard man—didn't like that very much, and if this punishment is reintroduced, I am convinced it will make criminals think twice. Once Joseph is free, I'm sure there will be lucrative newspaper offers to sell his story, but if he tells you that it wasn't painful or effective, I would take his answer with a pinch of salt. All you have to do is remember him as he is now, crying like a baby.

'While I tend to his wound, I want you to continue voting on my future. Do I give myself up or end it here on Thursday? The choice is yours.'

He turned off the webcam and pushed the trolley out of the cell, then untied Olemwu's left wrist and carried him back to a sitting position on his homemade commode, causing him to shriek with pain. He arched his back in an effort to get his backside off the box, but Gray pushed him back down and jerked his arm towards the ring on the wall, tying the rope securely. Once the shackles were back on Olemwu's ankles, he removed his belt from around the boy's knees.

'You said you were gonna treat my wounds.'

'Yeah, but then I remembered the kick on the chin, and now I can't be bothered. Don't worry, though, you will be free in a couple of days, maybe sooner.'

'But this will get infected,' Olemwu sobbed.

'You really want me to treat it? You really want some antiseptic on it?'

'Yes!' the boy shouted.

'Fine.' Gray left the cell and returned a moment later carrying the boy's underwear. He went round the back of the box and told the boy to lean forward as far as he could. Olemwu complied as best he could, and Gray applied the antiseptic to the boxer shorts and rubbed it into the wound.

The scream was ear splitting, much as Gray expected, but he carried on applying it nevertheless.

'What the fuck are you putting on there?' Olemwu shouted.

'Salt,' Gray said casually. 'It has antiseptic qualities, and I'm fresh out of Savlon.'

Olemwu continued cursing, but Gray had heard enough and ripped off a piece of tape, securing it over the boy's mouth.

'Ungrateful sod,' he said, leaving the cell and closing the door behind him. It was time to prepare his dinner, but first he headed upstairs for a bit more fresh air.

Chapter Twenty

Wednesday, 20 April 2011

Andrew Harvey woke just before six in the morning, and after getting his bearings, he turned on the television set in the small room of the bed and breakfast in Crowborough. The three men had stopped here to have dinner the previous evening and had been ordered to remain in the area after reporting in to Hammond.

'Find a place to rest up,' Hammond had said. 'If we get any news about Sally, I want you ready to move at a moment's notice.'

But there had been no news, just waiting, and late in the evening they had booked into separate rooms for the night.

Harvey turned to the BBC News channel, which was predictably still focusing on the Tom Gray saga. Live video from their correspondent at the scene showed the old factory building in the background as he explained what had happened during the night, which was absolutely nothing. However, he was looking ahead to the prospect of Gray handing himself in to the authorities, and he began speculating as to whether or not the government would agree to hold a referendum on Gray's justice bill.

What choice have they got? Harvey said to himself, and went to take a shower. Afterwards he shaved and dressed before calling the office for an update, only to be told the trail had gone cold. There were no hits with the other coach hire companies, with only a few dozen vehicles out on hire and the vast majority of those to regular customers. Of the remaining six, five had been pulled over by armed police officers, only to find the drivers and passengers were legitimate travellers on day trips, and the other one had been involved in a traffic accident on the M5 and had been towed to a garage, its passengers a group of casino staff returning from a day trip to the races.

They had also been unable to trace her phone, suggesting it had been turned off or destroyed, and an aerial search of the surrounding area had turned up nothing.

Harvey asked for updates on the Gray case and was told that Crawford from Norden Industries had reported over nine thousand canisters checked, but that still left over twenty-five thousand with only twelve hours to go.

They were also drawing a blank in the search for Gray's accomplices.

Twelve hours, he thought, *but only if Gray comes out this evening.* And even if he didn't, if he stayed in until Thursday, what difference would it make? One more criminal would get his just desserts, and maybe a handful of people would really give a shit.

Meanwhile Sally Clarkson, who had no field experience, was missing, assumed kidnapped by a terrorist cell. They just didn't have the people to deal with both, and as far as he was concerned, the Gray saga could run its course.

Sally was his priority now.

Why did Mansour have to turn up this week, of all weeks? If only he'd waited another few days, they would be fully resourced again. At the moment there just weren't enough people to deal with both Gray and ...

As the realisation hit him, he picked up his phone and dialled Hammond's mobile.

'John, I don't think it is a coincidence that Mansour turned up out of the blue. I think he's planning something in the next forty-eight hours.'

'What's his target?'

'That I don't know,' Harvey admitted, 'but fourteen months after being reported dead he suddenly appears on our radar, a mere twenty-four hours after Gray goes live on television. I think he knew we would be throwing everything at the Gray problem, allowing him to sneak in quietly and carry out his plan, whatever it is. If it hadn't been for Sally being so tenacious, he might have slipped clean past us.'

'There's been no traffic on the wires recently,' Hammond said. 'If something had been planned, we would have got a sniff of it by now.'

'I know, and that's what bothers me. None of the intelligence we have suggests an attack is imminent, yet everything points to him trying to exploit this window of opportunity. The only thing I would put any money on is that the target is somewhere near here, because they were heading towards the south coast when Sally was tailing them.'

'I concur. We'll work up possible targets from Tunbridge Wells down to Brighton and check with our American cousins to see what information they've forgotten to share with us.'

'Okay,' Harvey said. 'Once you've prioritised the targets, let me know and we'll head to the most likely. Oh, and speak to Hamad; see if he managed to get any hits on rented coaches.'

Harvey hung up and caught the introduction of the shadow home secretary on the news channel.

'Let's speak now to Michael Conway, who's just taken a seat in our Westminster studio. Thank you for joining us. Can you give us your reaction to Tom Gray's justice bill?'

'Over the last three years we have been looking at crime statistics, and frankly they make shocking reading. As Mr Gray has pointed out, in the last ten years this government have allowed over one hundred thousand career criminals to escape custodial sentences. And this is something we vow to change.

'We have been working on a set of proposals during this time, and much of what Mr Gray has asked for has already been covered. We have identified several locations to hold what we call super-prisons, each housing up to five thousand prisoners. To put that into context, the current largest prison in the UK, Wandsworth, holds less than seventeen hundred prisoners.

'Within these super-prisons we are looking into the possibility of implementing Mr Gray's suggestion that prisoners are kept in solitary confinement, and in Parliament last year we brought up the idea of prisoners being forced to work.'

'There are arguments that the government should be focusing on the causes of crime rather than building even more prisons. Do you think opting for an immediate custodial sentence is the right answer?'

The politician adjusted his posture and rearranged his jacket. 'We are not advocating immediate custodial sentences; I need to make that absolutely clear. What we plan to do is look at another of Mr Gray's proposals and examine the feasibility of clawing back some of the cost of policing. If we do this, a large percentage will go towards crime prevention in schools.

'We are confident that this approach will actually *reduce* the prison population in future years.'

'What about his other proposals?' the newscaster asked. 'Do you agree with the reintroduction of corporal punishment?'

'This issue has divided our party, I must admit. What we do propose is a one-year trial, and after that we will look at the results. Our ultimate aim is to eradicate recidivism, and we are determined to investigate all avenues.'

Harvey watched for another couple of minutes, then turned the television off. Despite the rhetoric, he knew that the shadow home secretary was only saying what he thought the country wanted to hear in the run-up to the election. He wasn't the first politician to do a U-turn, and he certainly wouldn't be the last.

Needing something he could trust beyond doubt, he collected his colleagues and went down for a full English breakfast.

———◡———

Sally Clarkson was jerked awake by the sound of the bedroom door opening. She knew instinctively that she was naked and tried to curl up in an attempt at modesty, but her hands and feet were tied to the corners of the wooden bed frame, and memories of the previous evening came flooding back.

Flynn had brought her here shortly after Mansour had questioned her. She had been dragged up the narrow stairs and bundled onto the bed, where the Irishman had removed her hood. He had tied rope around her right wrist, and she'd struggled when he tried to attach the other end to the bed frame, but several agonising punches to her kidneys and thighs had subdued her. Before long, all four limbs were secure and Flynn had left, only to return a few minutes later with a pair of scissors, which he'd used to slowly cut the clothes away from her body in some kind of sick, perverted strip tease. He'd taken his time over this, a full fifteen minutes, his breath quickening with each piece of flesh revealed.

In contrast, once she was naked, he had stripped off his own clothes as if they were on fire. He'd climbed clumsily on top of her, entering her painfully and thrusting wildly until reaching his climax a minute later.

He'd gone downstairs after that, returning a couple of hours after night had fallen for more of the same. This time he'd lasted longer and had left her with an aching body and the lingering odour of sweat and beer.

Finally alone again, sleep had not come easily, drifting in and out of semi-consciousness as she tried to foresee a way out of the situation, but it looked hopeless. She didn't have the strength to break her bonds, and it was unlikely he would free her, but the most damning realisation was that he had removed her hood, allowing her to see his face. She knew it was highly unlikely that she would live to tell anyone what he looked like. Her only hope was to survive as long as possible and pray that someone would find her.

As Flynn came through the door, she tried to force a smile onto her face, hoping to convince him to keep her around for a little while longer. The smile appeared more like a grimace, but it did nothing to dampen his ardour. She could see the bulge in his trousers as he came to stand next to her, and he followed her eyes, a sneer appearing on his face as he unzipped his pants and began to caress himself.

'What are you waiting for?' she asked, as alluringly as she could manage. 'Don't waste it.' She thrust her pelvis towards him, catching him off guard. He hadn't expected compliance, and he found himself suddenly embarrassed, standing before her with his dick in his hand.

The sneer was replaced by a look somewhere between confusion and anger, and he rushed from the room, tucking his manhood away.

Sally cursed to herself. How stupid could she be? He didn't want a girlfriend; he wanted someone to dominate, someone he could control and use at his leisure. Instead of prolonging her life, she had no doubt brought the end closer.

All she could do now was wait and hope she hadn't pissed him off too much.

Tom Gray pushed the trolley into Joseph Olemwu's cell and removed the tape from his hostage's mouth.

'Hungry?'

Olemwu shot him a filthy look. 'When I get outta here, I'm gonna fuck you up, old man.'

Gray was hurt and it showed on his face. He'd been called many things in his time, but *old*?

'Suit yourself.' He wheeled the trolley out and stood in the doorway, studying the boy before him.

'I have to ask, what have you learnt from the last few days?'

Olemwu continued to stare, his expression still hostile, but Gray gave him a few minutes to reply and rephrased the question when none was forthcoming.

'Has this experience taught you anything?'

'Yeah, it taught me to hate white fuckers like you,' Olemwu spat.

'Hmm. I was thinking more along the lines of "crime doesn't pay". You could have easily found a job, but you prefer to inflict misery instead. Even after all you've been through these past few days, your attitude still stinks.

'I had hoped to scare some sense into you, but it looks like you're a lost cause.'

'So what—you gonna kill me now? That's your answer to everything.'

'No,' Gray said, 'I'm not going to kill you. I'll let you go when this is all over, because I think you're just angry at the moment. When you get home, spend a couple of days with your mother, listen to what she says and think about what you want from your life.

'If you choose to carry on as you have so far, you will be in prison or dead within a very short time, and that would devastate your mother. Your father ... ' He shrugged, 'I'm not so sure.'

'I don't need you tellin' me how to live my life.'

'That's fine,' Gray said, his voice calm. 'I just wanted you to know that I'm giving you another chance.'

He pulled off a length of tape and placed it over the boy's mouth. 'Think about it.'

Gray left the cell and closed the door before turning the sound up on the television. It was approaching midday, and the government were due to announce its decision on his justice bill.

He considered giving Boyle Olemwu's food, but the thought was fleeting, and he tucked into the Spam and cold potatoes as he watched the news channel. The weather girl said he could expect rain for much of the day, but the forecast for the weekend was a return to the bright sunshine the country had enjoyed over the last few weeks.

Sounds good, he thought. *Maybe a trip to the beach when this is all over.*

The newscaster read out the main headlines, the first of which was an interview with the home secretary.

The politician sat in the Westminster studio and didn't look all that comfortable to Gray. When he began his announcement, he realised why.

'Unfortunately, Sharon, we have not been able to make a decision on a referendum at this time,' he said. 'The legal implications have to be considered and we don't want to make a promise to the people that we might have to break.'

Why not? Gray wondered. It wouldn't be the first time.

'We have a legal team looking into the possibility of implementing some or all of Mr Gray's proposals, but we cannot guarantee that any changes can be made to current legislation.'

'What are the sticking points?' the newscaster asked.

'Well, the Human Rights Act is fundamental in ensuring we live in a fair society, and it isn't as simple as repealing it. The Act was introduced to prevent people having to seek redress at the European Court of Human Rights, which takes up a lot of time and money. Even if the Act is torn up, people would still be able to take their case to Strasbourg and we would be bound by any judgement handed down.

'The only alternative would be to opt out of the Convention, but as the European Union itself is about to join as a party in its own right, it would mean pulling out of the EU as well.

'So you see, this isn't as simple as Mr Gray would have us all believe.'

'Which aspects of the Act are you most concerned about?'

'Protection from torture and mistreatment is the only real sticking point. The reintroduction of the birch would be a breach of Article Three.'

'We had the shadow home secretary on the programme this morning, and he seems convinced that this wouldn't be a problem.'

The minister couldn't wait to score a few political points at his counterpart's expense. 'I think you'll find that if you look at the current polls, my learned friend's party are in a very poor position. The comments you heard this morning were those of a party desperate for votes in the upcoming election, a party who hasn't thought the situation through, a party destined to disappoint the electorate if they ever get to power.'

'What about the part of the Act guaranteeing protection from slavery and forced labour? Isn't Mr Gray asking that prisoners be forced to work while they are incarcerated?'

'Not quite, Sharon. For one, he is suggesting that those who are willing to work will have their sentences reduced. In addition, the Act doesn't apply to prisoners carrying out work as part of their sentence.'

The newscaster nodded, looking at her notes. 'When can we expect a decision, Mr Home Secretary?'

'We believe we can make an announcement late on Friday.' he said.

'We expect this situation to be over by then. Won't that be too late?'

'Not at all. Mr Gray pointed out that we were not making a decision to appease him; we are making a decision based on the will of the people, and we want to make sure it is one that is right for the people.'

Gray turned the television off and picked up his mobile, selecting a preset number.

'Harvey,' the voice said.

'Hello, Andrew.'

'Tom. What can I do for you?'

'The home secretary isn't taking me seriously, Andrew. You know what that means.'

The phone went silent in Harvey's hand, and he checked to make sure he still had a signal, but Gray came back on the line a few moments later.

'Andrew, the next sound you hear will be Stuart Boyle.'

Gray placed the phone on the feeding trolley and pushed it into Boyle's cell so that Harvey could hear everything. From the corner of the room, he picked up a contraption that looked like a giant nutcracker, two 3-foot lengths of metal hinged together at one end, and he noted the look of fear in Boyle's eyes.

On the day Boyle had arrived, Gray had explained the reason for his abduction.

'My name is Tom Gray, father of Daniel Gray and husband to Dina Gray. On January 21st last year, you killed my son—which in turn led to the death of my wife—and at some point in the coming days you are going to pay for that.'

'What are you going to do to me? Are you going to kill me?' the boy had asked, the fear and panic in his voice palpable.

'No,' Gray had promised. 'Death is too quick, too easy. If I put a bullet through your head, you won't suffer at all; you'll just cease to be.

'No, you aren't going to die, no matter how much you beg me.'

He had explained the purpose of the implement and placed it inside the room so that Boyle could see it every waking moment. He hadn't said when it would be used, only that it wouldn't be straight away.

Now the time had come.

Gray placed the device around Boyle's left arm, a couple of inches above the wrist, holding it there while studying his captive's face. The boy was shaking, his eyes as big as saucers, and he was trying to say something. Gray removed the tape covering his mouth.

'Please, Mister, I'm so sorry ... '

Gray clamped his hand over Boyle's mouth and put his lips close to the boy's ear so that Harvey couldn't hear what he was about to say.

'Save it,' he growled softly. 'Sorrow isn't something you can express with a single word, it's something you feel inside. My solicitor told me that you were laughing and joking with your family when you walked free from court seven months ago. You even went on to commit more crimes, showing no remorse whatsoever for the pain you inflicted.

'You think you're sorry? Oh, believe me, you will be.'

Gray grasped both handles and squeezed them together with all the strength he could muster, crushing Boyle's radius and ulna like he was breaking into a crab claw. The sound emanating from Boyle's mouth barely managed to drown out the sound of the bones cracking.

Ignoring the screams, Gray transferred to the other side, inflicting similar damage to the right arm.

Boyle was a mess, snot and tears streaming down his face.

'Had enough?' Gray asked, his voice calm.

Boyle could hardly control his movements, only barely able to nod his head once.

'Yes,' he whimpered.

'Tough.'

Gray turned his attentions to Boyle's legs, shattering first the right tibia and fibula, followed by the left.

Once he'd finished, he picked up the phone and walked out of the cell, leaving the babbling Boyle to deal with the pain in his own way.

'That was for failing to meet the deadline. If I don't hear an announcement about the referendum on the news by six this evening, he's really gonna start hurting.'

'Whatever you did, you just went too far,' Harvey said. 'The home secretary put his neck on the line to arrange this deal, and you're doing all you can to jeopardise it.'

'The same home secretary that took all the credit when I released the hostage, adding a couple of points to the government's rankings in the latest MORI poll? Christ, with a couple of minutes of spin, this will be forgotten by the end of next week. He's got plenty of time to make up a story.'

'I hardly think—'

'Have you got kids, Andrew?'

'No,' Harvey said.

'Well, let me tell you, if you put a thousand fathers in my position, right now, half of them would do what I've just done.'

'What about the other half?'

'The other half would have killed him by now.'

'I don't think so, Tom. Think about it, how many kids are killed each year? It must be hundreds, but this is the first time anyone has taken the law into their own hands.'

'That's rubbish,' Gray said. 'There will have been quite a few revenge beatings over the years, but very few, if any, make the news. And besides, this hasn't been about a personal vendetta; it has been about raising awareness of the inequalities of justice and getting the law changed so that appropriate sentences are handed down, and the courts take into account the suffering of the victim for a change.'

'You sound convincing, Tom, and many would believe you, but I'm beginning to think that this was all about getting even with Stuart Boyle from the start.'

Gray sighed. 'Andrew, we've already been through this. I could have grabbed him any time I liked, and I reckon I could have gotten away with it if I'd put as much thought into it as I have into what I'm doing now. One thing I will concede, though, is that he was never going to just walk out of here. Whether this ends today or lasts until tomorrow night, he was always going to get a gentle reminder about his future conduct.'

Harvey had to admire the composure of the guy. He'd just mangled the kid, yet he sounded like a Sunday school teacher who'd just chastised a four-year-old for wearing a cap in church.

'That didn't sound gentle to me,' he said.

'Relax. I just gave him some thinking time, that's all. He won't be able to do much for the next couple of months except reflect on what happened here this week, and hopefully he will come to the right decision as to where his future lies.'

'It sounds like he needs medical attention,' Harvey said, Boyle's moans clearly audible in the background. 'I think it would be best to let him go now.'

'He'll be fine. In the meantime, I'd advise you to pass my message on to the home secretary.'

Gray turned the phone off and returned to Boyle's cell. He wasn't doing very well, the noise subsiding but his body shaking with the amount of adrenalin coursing through his veins. Gray checked him for shock but saw none of the signs: His pulse was fast yet strong; his skin wasn't cold or clammy; and his breathing, while rapid, wasn't shallow.

'You'll live,' he said, and put a new piece of tape over his mouth. He turned to leave the cell but stopped in the doorway, looking over his shoulder. With malice aforethought, he turned back and gave Boyle a Chinese burn, just to make sure he got the message.

Chapter Twenty-One

Carl Levine steered the narrow boat slowly towards the bank and cut the engine as it glided up to its mooring. He jumped ashore and tied it up securely, then climbed back on board to make sure everyone was ready to leave.

'It's pissing down outside,' he said as he entered the cabin, even though this was obvious from the rhythmic drumming on the roof of the boat.

'Good, gives us an excuse to keep our hoods up,' Tris Barker-Fink observed.

The eight men packed away the last of their belongings and sat down to wait for the minibus, which turned up just after half past one in the afternoon. While Levine went to hand the boat back, the others took their baggage and climbed aboard, Jeff Campbell taking the seat next to the driver.

The driver was a Geordie in his early thirties, with receding hair and a photo of two kids, stuck to the middle of his steering wheel. He smiled and introduced himself as Barry, but as he studied his passenger, his expression changed, concern registering on his face. As their mug shots had been all over the media for the last thirty-six hours, Campbell was expecting just this kind of reaction, and he put his hand inside his jacket pocket.

He withdrew his hand slowly, and it took all his will power to stop himself from exploding with laughter: Barry looked like he was torn between running for his life and shitting his pants, having recognised his fares. The look changed to confusion when Campbell revealed a wad of notes.

'Here we go, Barry,' he said, counting off five hundred in twenties. 'That's a little tip for you. The thing is, I'm going to need your mobile, and I'm afraid we can't be stopping along the way, so if you need to go, go now. One of my friends will escort you to the toilet.'

Barry shook his head, mouth still dangling open, so Campbell asked about the fuel situation. It turned out they had nearly a full tank, and Barry assured him it would last them all the way to Leeds.

'Sorry, Barry, change of plans. I know we said Leeds when we ordered the bus, but we're actually going south. Just a precaution, you understand.'

Barry nodded this time, but when he learned of their new destination he still didn't think they would need to stop for diesel. He continued to stare at Campbell, expecting him to pull out a weapon at any moment.

Jeff smiled. 'Chill out, Barry. We're not ruthless killers, and we aren't going to hurt you. Just concentrate on the driving, and it'll all be over in a few hours. You'll probably be interviewed by the papers afterwards, as well as the news channels. Should earn you a few extra quid.'

Barry seemed to perk up at that idea, and it helped him find his voice.

'Did you really kidnap all them thieves?' he asked.

'We can't talk about that, I'm afraid.'

'Why not? I thought they were going to let you off, like.'

'Maybe,' Campbell said, 'but we haven't got anything in writing yet, and anything you tell the police could be held against us.'

'Fair enough,' the driver said, 'but if it *was* you, then me and about twenty million others would love to buy you guys a pint. You're the bee's knees, real fucking heroes. Not just because of what you did for that Tom guy, but just for being in the SAS. Man, you guys rock. You're like fucking Superman or sumpin'.'

'No we're not,' Paul Bennett said from the seat behind the driver. 'We're just well trained, well disciplined and very fit. We don't leap tall buildings in a single bound or take on a thousand armed enemies and kill them with a small knife and a single mag of ammo. That's the stuff of books and movies.'

Barry turned to face him, undeterred. 'Well, *I* think you're heroes. I've been burgled and had me satnav nicked twice in the last four months. What's happening to these toe rags is fucking brilliant. I mean it. There's even a petition on the government website to let Tom off if he turns himself in. I tell ya, the whole country loves 'im, except for the fucking criminals. There's already over a million signatures on it, and it's growing all the time.'

'A million?' Campbell asked, quite incredulous.

'Aye. And me and the wife have signed it, and me mates at work. Listen, I fancy meself as a writer. I'd love to hear some of your war stories for me book. It's a bit like them other SAS stories but better, like.'

At that moment Carl Levine returned from the boat office and climbed in the back, but Campbell motioned for him to get back out, and he joined him outside the bus.

'You sit up front with the driver,' he said.

'Why?' Levine asked.

'Because you are the least likely to be recognised if anyone is coming towards us.'

Levine realised this was good thinking on Jeff's part, particularly if they went through any cameras capable of facial recognition. It was good to see that the old team was still on the ball.

Barry set off as soon as Levine put his seatbelt on and immediately began to press him for anecdotes. He turned to look at the smiling Campbell, who simply offered a shrug which said 'I told you we should have tied him up and left him on the boat.'

Carl Levine sat back and thought about the conflicts he had been involved in, from Northern Ireland to Iraq and Afghanistan. He'd risked life and limb on more than one occasion, had fought his way out of impossible situations and suffered some serious injuries in his time.

After weighing everything up, he knew this was going to be the most difficult three hours of his life.

A few minutes after Harvey had relayed Gray's message to Hammond, his boss was back on the phone.

'We've got a possible location,' Hammond said without preamble. 'The chopper spotted a coach at a farm house near Cuckfield, and there's a lot of heat sources inside the barn.'

'Give me the address,' Harvey said, and Hammond relayed the details which he punched into his satnav.

'I'm about fifteen minutes away. Who else is en route?'

'We have Sussex Armed Response vehicles on the way. They should get there at about the same time.'

'Okay. I'll let you know what we find.'

Harvey cut the connection and let the speed of his Vauxhall creep up to eighty as he barrelled past other vehicles on the A23. He'd been out filling the car when Gray's call had come in, not because he was short on fuel but simply as an excuse to get out of the stuffy bed and breakfast and clear his mind. Some people liked the solitude of a hot, foamy bath to do their thinking; others liked background music to get the mental juices flowing. But with Harvey it was driving.

Although his focus should have been on finding Sally, he would suddenly find himself thinking about Gray again. He didn't know why, but something was niggling away at the back of his mind. He thought it might be because he was trying to imagine what Gray had done to Stuart Boyle, but he dismissed that idea. No, some-thing wasn't adding up with this whole affair, but he struggled to put his finger on it.

Before he knew it, he was off the dual carriageway and less than two miles from his destination, so he cast aside all thoughts of Tom Gray and focused on the job in hand.

The Tactical Firearms Unit had made good time and was waiting a few hundred yards from the farm, which lay just over a small rise. The officers were already out of their vehicles; two Volvo estates and three unmarked cars. Most were donning their gear and checking their weapons, while a senior officer gave instructions.

Harvey climbed out and introduced himself, and was told that a scouting team had already been sent out. 'One is heading up that hill there to get a view of the back of the farmhouse,' Chief Inspector Roberts said, pointing to a figure dressed in black mak-ing his way to the vantage point. Harvey could just about see the chimney of the farmhouse from where he stood, so the armed of-ficer should have a good view of the entire farm once he reached his position.

'Do we know how many are in there?' Harvey asked.

'Thermal imaging from the chopper shows thirty-six. We did a drive-by in an unmarked car but saw no one outside. Two officers are following the hedgerow to the gate, and once my men are suited up, we'll send two unmarked cars to the other end of the lane. At the moment we only want to maintain a perimeter and gather as much intel as we can. If need be, we'll call in backup.'

'What about to the east of the farm? Have you got any men there?'

'There's nothing to the east except fields,' the chief inspector said. 'If anyone makes off that way, we can quickly round them up, and the chopper will keep tabs on anyone making a run for it.'

Harvey looked up, and for the first time heard the faint buzz of the force helicopter as it maintained its position above the area.

The sound was barely audible out in the open air, so it was doubtful that anyone inside could hear it.

'Are you patched in to the chopper?'

'We have comms and video feed,' the officer said, and offered Harvey a seat in his car, out of the rain. He produced a tablet PC, its seven-inch screen showing exactly what the chopper observer was seeing. A touchscreen menu on the right allowed them to toggle through the light spectrum, from visible to infrared.

'It uses a microwave frequency to provide real-time images from the eye in the sky, really handy for this kind of operation.'

'I didn't know they could actually look into buildings,' Harvey said. 'I mean, I've seen them on cop shows on TV, but all they showed was the outline of buildings. They were never like this.'

'That's the old technology. This works on the principal of Capability Brown's dictum that nature abhors a straight line. Special software takes each image apart pixel by pixel, and anything which represents a straight line, such as the wall of a building, or a window, is ignored. Only heat sources with irregular shapes are displayed. There's actually more to it than that, but you get the idea.'

'You normally just see stuff like this in the movies.'

'Well, you'd be surprised at how many movie ideas become reality. Some say the first flip-up mobile phone was modelled on the communicators from Star Trek.'

Harvey studied the screen, which showed white blobs representing the body heat of the people inside the barn. A few appeared to be stationary, others moving around slowly, as if mingling at a party.

'No one seems to be isolated,' he observed. 'I would have expected Sally to be kept apart from the rest of them.'

'I had the same thought, but we found no other heat sources apart from those in the barn. She might be in the main house, or it could mean she's ...'

He left the statement hanging, and Harvey knew he didn't think there was much hope of finding Sally alive. Nevertheless, if they went in, it had to be on the assumption that she was.

'Do you have any thermal cameras of your own, or are you relying on the chopper images?'

'We haven't the budget for them at the moment, but we hope to get some in the next financial year.'

Fat lot of good that will do us now, Harvey thought.

'What information do we have about the bus?'

'Hired four weeks ago, paid by credit card and collected two days ago,' Roberts told him.

'Doesn't sound like our guys, unless it was a cloned or stolen card. Even then, they would probably use it much closer to the time to avoid detection. This doesn't add up.'

Harvey tapped his fingers on the side of the seat, deep in thought. 'I'll need a gun,' he said. 'If this goes down soon, you'll need every available man.'

'My men can handle anything they're presented with,' Roberts said, dismissing the idea.

'Have it your way.' Harvey got on the phone to Hammond, and three minutes later the chief inspector got a call from his superiors. It only lasted a few seconds, and after hanging up, he opened the car's armoury and grudgingly handed over the Austrian pistol, a belt holster, two single-stack magazines and twenty 9mm rounds.

After loading the magazines, Harvey pulled the slide back to ensure it was clear, inserted a mag, hit the slide release to chamber a round and applied the safety. It took less than a minute to thread the holster onto his own belt, and he stowed the weapon, all the time keeping an eye on the images coming from the tablet PC.

Two of the unmarked cars set off to take up their positions farther up the road, and the officer on the hill reached the crest, lying up in the rain-sodden ground. After a quick scan through his binoculars, he reported back to the scene commander.

'Only two windows on this side of the building; both have their curtains closed. I can't see any movement.'

'Acknowledged. Charlie team, what's your status?'

'Charlie team in position, one hundred yards from the farm entrance. No sign of movement from here.'

'Roger that.'

'Now what?' Harvey asked.

'We wait. Once we know what we're up against, we can make a decision. First, though, we need to identify exactly who we're dealing with.'

'Well, we can't do that sitting in here. I'm going to take a closer look.'

'I can't allow that, Mr Harvey.'

Harvey already had his hand on the door release. 'If we wait for them to come out, we could be sitting here for days. Let me get in close and ID them; then you can decide what to do.'

Roberts was about to object again, but Harvey stopped him short. 'If you want to sit and read the Health and Safety manual, that's fine, but while there's a chance my colleague is in there, I want to go and take a look. You can either tag along, or I can call my boss again. I don't want to have to do that because it could cost you your job, but we have good reason to believe an attack is going to take place in the next twenty-four hours, and there simply isn't time to do things by the book.'

Roberts knew it wasn't an empty threat and that there was more to be gained from playing along than making waves. There was certainly a lot to lose if he stood in the spook's way, and he hadn't risen this high by making bad decisions.

'Okay, on your head be it. The chopper has done a three-sixty of the area, and the best way to approach is from up on the hill, where Simpson is keeping watch. There's a large window on the ground floor and a smaller window on the first floor. Once you've had a good look at the house and the barn, get back here, preferably without losing the element of surprise.'

Harvey let the last comment slide: if he'd been in Roberts's position he would probably have said something a little more cutting.

'I'll need comms,' he told the officer.

'We haven't got any. They are issued at the station, and we don't carry spares.'

Harvey thought for a moment. 'Give me your mobile number.'

He typed in the digits as Roberts recited them and hit the 'Call' button. 'Answer it and leave the connection open,' Harvey said, climbing out of the warm car and into the teeming rain, turning his collar up as drops ran down his neck.

The climb would have been a doddle in dry weather, but the underfoot conditions made walking a nightmare, and he slipped a dozen times before he reached the summit. He tapped Officer Simpson on the shoulder and began the climb down the other side, the descent a lot faster than the ascent. When he reached the bottom, he moved to the wall of the house as fast as the conditions would allow and crouched down under the window. With his right hand he drew his weapon, and with his left he reached into his pocket and pulled out his phone.

'I'm at the window, but I can't hear anything,' he whispered into the handset.

'Roger that,' Roberts replied.

Harvey stuck his head up, looking for a gap that would afford him a glance into the room, and he found one in the bottom right-hand corner. He peeped through but saw no sign of movement, so he moved to the end of the wall and gauged the distance to the barn. It appeared to be no more than forty yards away—maybe four or five seconds on a good day—but the rain had turned the ground to thick mud, and it wouldn't be easy going.

He decided to take the long way round, moving first behind a tractor, then finding cover behind a Land Rover a few yards away. He stopped to survey the area, but saw no movement from either the barn or the house. The next piece of cover was a muck-spreading machine, and once he made his way there, he had only open ground to the barn. The distance was down to about twenty yards, and he covered it as fast as he could, nearly losing his balance twice.

He was at the rear of the barn, which was solidly built from slats of wood nailed vertically to a wooden frame. Finding a way to look inside wasn't going to be easy. He quickly checked the planks but couldn't find a gap between any of them, so he headed round the side, hidden from any prying eyes in the house. Here he had more time to explore and found a knothole at waist height. Peering inside, he was met with a wall of darkness, but he could hear muffled voices. He moved farther along the wall, all the time checking for the slightest gap, and he eventually found one right on the corner. He knelt down to look through the two-inch hole and clearly saw the occupants.

Holstering the gun, he stood up and spoke into the phone. 'Pull your men back. These aren't the people we're looking for.'

'Who's in there?' Roberts asked.

'I don't know, but unless our targets managed to age forty years and have a sex change in the last twenty-four hours, this isn't them. It looks like some sort of local produce fair. They're probably inside because of the rain.'

Rather than risk climbing back up the hill, Harvey walked out of the farm's main entrance and caught a lift back to his car.

Chapter Twenty-Two

Abdul Mansour had been putting his men through their paces since six that morning, and they all knew their responsibilities. After nine hours of practice, it was time for a meal—the last one for most, he knew—and then they would begin the last leg of their journey.

With no suitable cooking facilities available, they had sent two cars into town to purchase soft drinks, cold meats and bread. Not the most elegant of banquets, but it was enough to give them the energy they would need in the coming hours.

Mansour ate his share while once again studying the men around him. The ones who had weapons experience had done a good job teaching the novices, and now every man could change a magazine within five seconds, and all knew the drill for clearing a blockage. It was unfortunate that they couldn't conduct any live fire exercises, as that would have given him a true indication of their ability to handle the rifles, and he expected many to panic when the time came, but he had chosen the best to lead the fire from the ridge, and as long as they cleared a path for the riders, that was all that mattered. The rest would rain down chaos and confusion, and the undermanned police force would not know which way to turn.

Popping the last slice of cold mutton into his mouth, he went down to the cellar to add the finishing touches to the two vests the riders would wear. The C4 explosive was in place, as were the detonators. All he needed to do now was attach the wiring from the detonators to the wire leading to the vibration device of an unregistered pay-as-you-go mobile phone, so that when he called the number, the electrical charge would instead set off the smaller charge, which would trigger the bigger explosion.

He could have attached them earlier, but even though no one knew the number, these modern dialling machines could accidentally trip across the numbers and set off the vests prematurely.

With the numbers pre-programmed into his own unregistered phone against the colours each rider would be wearing—black and red—he made the connections and carried the vests up the stairs. As he reached the top, he heard the sound of a ringtone and placed the vests carefully on the floor, his body tensing as the anger took hold.

'Who has a phone?' he shouted, and all eyes turned to him. Then slowly they all turned their heads to look at one of the men at the back of the barn.

Mansour strode over and snatched the phone from him, looking for the 'Off' switch. He couldn't immediately find one, so he thrust it back into the man's hand.

'Turn it off, now!'

Ibrahim Mohammed sheepishly took the Smartphone and did as instructed, then handed it back to Mansour.

'I said no mobile phones, didn't I?'

He looked around the room and the general consensus was that Ibrahim had fucked up badly, and it showed on their faces.

'Who else has a phone?' Mansour demanded.

No one spoke, so he turned to Ibrahim. 'Why did you bring this?' he asked, barely trying to disguise the anger in his voice.

'I didn't bring it, brother; it belonged to the woman.'

Mansour almost turned purple, the vein in his temple throbbing. 'How stupid can one person be?' he shouted. 'Every secret service agent in this country is looking for that woman, and you turn on her phone and lead them straight to us!'

'I'm sorry, brother, I—'

Ibrahim didn't manage to finish the sentence due to the knife protruding from the front of his throat. Mansour withdrew the blade and watched as he collapsed to the floor, clutching at the wound, blood pouring between his fingers.

Abdul watched until he took his last breath, then turned to the others.

'That is the last time anyone disobeys me. Is that clear?'

There were nods all round, and their expressions told him that they were obviously shocked at the sudden explosion of violence. This didn't bode well for the coming battle, but there wasn't time to do anything about it.

'Everyone, pack up your things and be ready to leave in the next five minutes. You two,' he said, pointing to the riders standing next to their bikes, 'come with me and I will show you how the vests work.'

The men followed him, and he dressed each one in turn, then showed them how to operate the trigger. It was a small device, much like a lipstick container, with a red button on the top. A twenty-inch length of wire ran from the trigger to the first of the detonators, then spread out like a spider's web to connect to the other detonators embedded in the twenty packs of explosives, ten on the front of each vest and another ten on the back. Each block of C4 was the size of a Snickers bar, and he had studded them all with nails in order to cause the maximum amount of collateral damage.

'Put your jackets on and keep them zipped up. We don't want anyone seeing the explosives before we even get there.'

Mansour turned to address the others. 'I want to make sure you all know the route. Sami, where do we meet up?'

'At the Hare and Hounds pub on the A272.'

'Good. Zulfir, how do we get there?'

'Follow the A22 to the Black Down roundabout, then take the first left towards Haywards Heath. At the next roundabout take the first left, signposted Newick, then follow the signs for the A272 for another six miles.'

'Excellent. Has everyone got that?' Everyone offered a single nod.

'I want a couple of cars between each of us, and those in the back seats should keep your heads down as much as possible. They will probably be looking for a coach, but if they see thirty men in convoy it could give us away.

'Brothers, our time has come. Be strong. Be brave. Allah will be watching over us.

'Allahu Akbar!'

'Allahu Akbar!' they chorused.

When the call came in, Harvey was just leaving a convenience store, having picked up a sandwich for a late lunch. He was still pissed that he had been forced to return the Glock, but as he had separated from the Tactical Firearms Unit, he could hardly go gallivanting around the countryside with a weapon they were responsible for.

The display said the call was from Hammond, and he hit the 'Accept' button.

'We've found Sally,' his boss said. 'She's at a farm seven miles north of Eastbourne.'

'Another wild goose chase?' Harvey asked, not relishing another crawl up a muddy hill.

'Not this time. Her phone was activated for just under three minutes, then went dead again. GCHQ pinpointed her location, and the tactical firearms unit are on their way. Meet them at these coordinates.'

Hammond began to reel the numbers off, but Harvey stopped him. 'John, the armed response vehicles are all well and good for domestic standoffs, but this is different. We need someone with a lot more experience in hostage situations. The boys from Hereford, to be exact.'

'I've already been in touch with them, but it will take them five hours to deploy, and there are signs that Mansour and his team have been at the farm, but the chopper only saw two faint heat sources, which means they've moved on. If Mansour is going to make his hit today, five hours is just too long.'

'What about the team deployed to tackle Gray? He's probably going to be coming out in the next four hours, so is it really necessary to have them there?'

Hammond was silent for a while, weighing up the options, but he came to the same conclusion as his subordinate.

'Okay, I'll get in touch with their commanding officer and get back to you. In the meantime, take these details down and get moving.'

Harvey asked him to wait while he got back into his car, then punched the location into the satnav. He was looking at a thirty-minute drive, and the SAS would be facing a slightly longer journey.

'I want to meet up with the Tactical Firearms Unit on the way and grab some of their kit,' Harvey said. 'Their tablet PC link to the local police chopper will be handy for a tactical overview. It would also help if you can get hold of a handheld thermal camera for the takedown. I think I saw one mentioned in one of the daily reports from SO15. Can you check on that?'

'I'll call them and find out. If they haven't got one, we'll source one from somewhere,' Hammond promised.

Harvey asked him to make sure the Sussex Police helicopter got above the scene as soon as possible, then set off through the driving rain.

The timing of the discovery couldn't have been worse, the streets and lanes packed with parents picking their kids up from school. It was bad enough in fine weather, but during downpours it was always bedlam, with three times as many vehicles on the road, and most of them people carriers.

What he thought would be a half-hour journey was going to take at least twice as long, and he still had to meet up with the Tactical Firearms Unit. First, though, he had to get out of this traffic jam and onto open road.

He called Roberts and arranged to meet a couple of miles away, and the officer was waiting when he pulled up to the hotel car park. Harvey got into the police car and Roberts handed him a tablet PC, making sure Harvey knew how to use it.

'I'm sorry about earlier,' Harvey said as he was getting out. 'I was a bit harsh going over your head.'

'Don't mention it. Roles reversed, I would probably have done the same myself.'

Harvey conceded the point and ran back to his own car, sending spray flying as he sped onto the main road.

During the journey he received a call from Hammond, who gave him new coordinates for the rendezvous and confirmed that the team he was meeting had already picked up the thermal camera from SO15.

Traffic had thinned with the end of the school run, and he managed to catch up a little time, but still arrived ten minutes behind Blythe and his men.

He wasn't surprised to see only eight of them, as he had been a fan of the SAS since he'd purchased a copy of *Bravo Two Zero* in the early nineties. There had been no Internet for him to do more research on them when he was thirteen, but he had found a plethora of books at his local library and had read everything from their formation by David Stirling in 1941, their exploits in the Dhofar rebellion, right through to the Iranian Embassy siege on the fifth of May 1980 and their much understated presence in the Falkland conflict of 1982.

They were all parked up in a field a mile from the target, their two Land Rovers hidden from view by an overgrown hedge which lined the road. Harvey's car had struggled to join up with them after entering the field, its tyres more suited to concrete than sodden grass.

The men before him represented two 4-man patrols and had been through the rigorous counterrevolutionary warfare training, which included expert training in close quarter battle, hostage rescue and siege breaking. Rather than the black uniform normally associated with the SAS, they wore normal fatigues, the disruptive pattern material more suited to the current surroundings.

A glance up through the stinging rain confirmed that Hotel 900, the Sussex Police helicopter, was on station.

'What's the plan?' Harvey asked Blythe.

'Willard has gone ahead with the thermal-imaging camera and will let us know where the X-rays are, and the best angle from which to approach the building. We'll be setting off to join him in the next few minutes.'

'Okay. Wanna take a seat in your Land Rover and view the aerial picture?'

Blythe nodded and they escaped the rain, ensuring the tablet PC didn't get wet. The picture showed one very faint heat sign in the barn and only a couple of faint sources in the farm building itself. Two of the white blobs appeared to be lying down, with only one moving around. Looking farther afield, they saw hedges on three sides of the farm that would provide them cover from view, at least until they made the assault, but there were no further signs of human life. A few animals were seen, but nothing large enough to be a person in disguise.

'Looks like they already left,' Blythe said, 'but one of these two prone figures could be your colleague.'

'Then we go in and get her.'

'Not "we",' Blythe told him, "us". 'You stay here and set up a road block, see if we can catch the others.'

Harvey looked surprised, like he'd just been slapped in the face. 'The girl in there is my responsibility,' he said. 'I'm not here to organise the traffic cops.'

'You're not coming with us, period. We don't work like that. We work hard and train hard, and I'm not having one of my operations going tits up because some spook thinks he's John McLean.'

'But—'

'No "buts". You stay here. You'll have comms, and you can keep us updated on their positions using the chopper view, but you're not joining the takedown.'

Harvey pulled out his phone and hit the speed dial for Hammond. 'John, can you get on to the MoD and have a word—'

Blythe grabbed the phone from his grasp and put it to his ear, ignoring Harvey's protestations. 'This is Major Sean Blythe. Who am I speaking to?'

'Sean, it's John. We spoke earlier.'

'Well, John, we have a problem. As the team leader, we go on my say-so, and my say-so only. Either tell your boy to pull his neck in and let us do our job, or we withdraw and he can go in by himself.'

'Let me speak to him.'

Blythe handed the phone over, no emotion on his face. Harvey took it and listened to his superior.

'Andrew, you asked for these people because you know they are the best at what they do. It's time to swallow your pride and let them get on with their job.'

It wasn't his pride that was the issue; it was the knowledge that once this was over, his ten-year career would be, too. If he could come out of this with some distinction, he might be able to salvage something, but as Hammond pointed out, these were the best men for the job, and he was more likely to be a hindrance than a help. He realised that his desire to take part in the operation was not driven by the hope of saving Sally, but for his own selfish reasons, despite feeling responsible for her current position.

Besides, it was the Gray affair that had caused all the problems, and nothing he did in the next four hours was going to make up for the fact that he had been unable to prevent loss of life or injury to the hostages. That it was Gray who had put the home secretary in such an awkward political position wasn't his fault, but he knew he would be the one to take the blame.

'You're right, John. I'm sorry.'

Harvey hung up and apologised to Blythe, too, who brushed it aside as if the little episode had never taken place.

'I want you to organise road blocks for a twenty-mile radius. They can't have gotten that far in the last hour, so we start at twenty miles and squeeze it until we have them cornered.'

'Road blocks have already been set up,' Harvey told him. 'That's the first thing our team did.'

'What radius?'

'That I don't know,' Harvey admitted.

'Then find out, and make sure it's big enough that they couldn't have slipped through already. We need—'

He held up a finger as he listened to the message coming through on his earpiece. After a moment he tapped his throat microphone twice to acknowledge the message, then shared the details with Harvey.

'Willard says there are no X-rays moving in the barn, but the door is open and he can see a coach. That suggests they left in other transport. Pass that on to the police. They might just be looking for one vehicle.

'He also has two heat sources in the house, one on the ground floor and one on the first. The one on the first floor appears to be lying down. That's probably Sally.'

'I agree.'

Blythe handed over a comms set and showed Harvey how to use it, then gathered his men together and told them what they were up against. Within minutes they were on their way to meet up with Willard at the lying-up point, sticking close to the hedge in single file.

The LUP was behind a hedge three-feet high, roughly five hundred yards from the barn, to the right of which lay the farmhouse. They found Willard crouching down, viewing the scene through the budding foliage.

'Echo one,' Blythe said through his throat mike, using Harvey's call sign. 'We're at the LUP. Do you have an update on X-ray One's position?'

'I have you on the screen, and X-ray One is on the far side of the main building.'

X-ray One was the designation of the heat source that was mobile, the one least likely to be Sally. X-ray Two was the figure on the first floor, and X-ray Three was in the barn. Although Blythe and his team had their own thermal-imaging camera and were able to see which floor X-ray One was on, they only had a two-dimensional view of him, and no depth perception. Harvey, in turn, could only see where he was in relation to the inner walls. Together, however, they could build up a three-dimensional picture of the target's exact location.

'We need to take him alive so that we can find out what Mansour's target is.'

'If he cooperates, he'll live,' was all Blythe would commit to. Then he spoke to the four men who would make the initial approach. 'Take yourselves down the hedge line until you have the barn between yourselves and the farmhouse; then move across and clear it. Once the barn is secure, we'll move on the house.'

Edwards, Monk, Frost and Wickens moved off at a trot, and within two minutes they signalled that they were in position.

The other four would remain in reserve at the LUP, with Mitchell manning the HK417 medium-range sniper rifle.

'Echo One, any sign of movement in the barn?' Blythe asked.

'Negative,' Harvey replied, so he gave the word to move in.

The four men pushed their way through a gap in the hedge and covered the ground quickly, lining up against the side of the barn. Monk took the lead, rounding the corner and rushing through the opening, rifle raised, covering the right-hand side of the building. Edwards was next through, the barrel of the MP5SD suppressed submachine gun following his eyes as he scanned for signs of movement. They were followed quickly by Frost and Wickens, who moved past them and made their way to the back of the barn, where the heat source was known to be.

Frost raised his fist when he saw the feet sticking out from the front of the bus, and as he moved in closer, he kept his gun trained on the prostrate figure, even though the pool of blood around its head suggested it wasn't going to put up much of a fight.

'X-ray Three is dead,' he reported, and the others crowded round, two checking the body for signs of life and booby traps, while the others kept their weapons trained.

'Building clear,' Frost said. 'Where is X-ray One?'

'Still on the far side of the farm house. Move in now.'

Frost responded with two clicks of the throat mike and signalled to the others to move out. The plan was for Wickens and Frost to set charges on two of the ground-floor windows. They would detonate the first and send through CS canisters, and while the target was reeling from this, they would detonate the second charge, further disorientating him, allowing two of the team to burst through the door and make the takedown.

They were just setting the first shaped charge when the call came through.

'X-ray One is on the move, heading upstairs.'

Flynn had been torn between emotions since his encounter with the woman earlier that morning. His personal porn collection swayed towards the dominance and submission genre, and when this young filly had landed in his lap, he thought it was Christmas and all his birthdays come at once. Last night had been the first chance he had ever had to play out his fantasies, but this morning she had shattered those dreams.

At first he'd felt shame, like someone had walked in on him in mid-masturbation. In effect, that is what she had done, jumping into his fantasy without invitation and catching him unawares.

Next had come anger, a burning desire to punish her for ruining his morning. Not just this morning, but the days and weeks ahead. He had planned to keep her alive for as long as possible, but after this morning's performance, he wasn't so sure.

The final emotion had been lust, his loins leading his head, telling him to keep her around, just smack the confidence out of her. This emotion had won the day, and he had laid into her just after nine that morning, punctuating each slap with an instruction.

'Don't'—whack!—'ever'—slap!—'speak'—smack!—'to me'—whack!—'again!'

She had laid there sobbing, her left eye beginning to swell, and blood running from her nose, where she had moved her head mid-slap. She wasn't a pretty picture when he left her, and he realised he had done exactly what he asked the raghead not to do: damage her. After taking himself away to calm down, he had returned an hour later and was pleased to see her cowering this time. Regardless, she was still in a state, so he had untied her and allowed her to clean herself up, all the time demeaning her to make sure she understood that she was his slave now, that there was no friendship or pity involved. He made her change the bedding and scrub the mattress, getting rid of the piss-stained sheet and the smell that went with it.

After tying her up again, he had left her alone, but parted with a warning that he would be back for more later, and return he did, but only to release her left hand so that she could eat a meagre lunch. He knew this would increase her anxiety, and it appeared to work.

Leaving her for a couple of hours longer, he settled down to watch one of his favourite DVDs to get himself in the mood, but he was interrupted by the sound of the cars leaving in a hurry. He would have to dispose of the coach himself, but that wasn't a problem. *That can be done later this evening,* he thought. It was simply a case of driving it to the outskirts of the town two miles away and leaving it running. Some local pisshead would have it away in a matter of minutes, and no doubt it would be burnt out by the morning.

Once they were gone, he concentrated again on the movie. After years of practice he could bring himself close to climax again and again without going over the edge, and he was almost delirious as he climbed the stairs for the final explosive moment.

As squad leader, Frost would make the ultimate decision, and there just wasn't time to hold a Chinese parliament and get the opinions of the other three. They could try to make a noise and coax him downstairs again, but that would put him on his guard, and an X-ray on edge was not conducive to a good day. On the other hand, if they forced an entry while he was upstairs, he would have time to arm himself and either kill the hostage or kill one of Frost's men, neither of which option he could accept.

Peering through the kitchen window, he saw a mobile phone on the counter, and it gave him an idea, which he shared with the team.

He took off his respirator and put his ear to the glass in the back door. From the other end of the house, he heard the muffled shouts, which wasn't good for the hostage, but it should keep the X-ray occupied for a few moments. The door was old, paint flaking all around the frame, so he was very gentle when he tried the handle. At first he thought it was locked, but when he applied a little pressure, it gave with a creak.

Heart in his mouth, he was aware that the shouting had stopped. His hand went to the trigger guard of the MP5SD, ready to rush, but a moment later the verbal abuse started up again, much to his relief.

Removing one of his gloves, he crept into the kitchen and closed the door, then picked up the phone, flicking through the menu to the 'Sounds' option. He selected 'Ringtones,' then chose the current tune and put it back on the countertop near the sink, before retreating to a position behind the kitchen door.

A moment later he heard the sound of footsteps as the target rushed down the stairs and burst into the room, grabbing the phone. He had his back to Frost, so Frost couldn't see the look of confusion, but when he pounced he saw the surprise on the X-ray's face.

'Down on the floor! Now!'

Flynn spun round and stared in amazement at the soldier pointing the silenced weapon at him.

His first thought was that he was truly fucked.

His second was that it was the raghead's fault.

His third thought was to grab for the knife in the sink, and it was the last thought he ever had.

The first bullet smashed through his temple and pierced the brain as it continued its journey. By the time it hit the far side of the skull, it had lost so much momentum that it wasn't capable of breaking through the other side, so it just bounced around like a fly in a jar, shredding the brain even more.

The second bullet, fired less than a second later, wasn't necessary, but training dictated a double-tap, and that's what the X-ray got.

The other three members of the team burst in as he shouted his warning, but Flynn was on the floor before they got through the door, so they hurdled over him and raced through the kitchen door.

'X-ray One down,' Frost reported, his voice just a little taut after his first kill.

The squad cleared the house, room by room, ending up in the master bedroom, where they found Sally still tied to the bed, tears running down her face. They didn't know if they were tears of fear or joy, but as with most traumatic situations they knew they would continue for some time. They untied her and gently wrapped her in the bed sheet before escorting her down the stairs and into the front room, seating her on the sofa.

'House clear, X-ray One down, hostage safe,' Frost said over the comm link, his voice steadier now that the burst of adrenalin had been spent. 'She has a few injuries but nothing life-threatening. I'm more concerned about her mental state.'

Chapter Twenty-Three

Twelve miles from their destination, it might as well have been twelve thousand miles, because if he spent another minute in Barry's company, Carl Levine was sure he would kill him. The last three hours had been an absolute nightmare, and he'd lost count of the number of times he's said, 'That's classified'. Still, Barry was relentless, desperate for a firsthand account of a battle—or even a minor skirmish—for his book.

Eventually Levine had caved in and told him about the time he and three others had parachuted into Taliban territory in Afghanistan. They had marched forty miles in two nights, carrying a hundred pounds of kit each, then attacked an enemy stronghold, killing over a hundred and fifty men and rescuing a British soldier before carrying him the forty miles back to the pickup point.

Barry was lapping it up, but the others in the back could barely contain themselves. They knew for a fact that Carl had never been to Afghanistan and that no self-respecting squad leader would ever take three men on such a suicidal operation. Even when Paul Bennett started ribbing Levine about his exploits, Barry just thought it was friendly regimental banter.

Their destination was a holiday cottage two miles from Gray's stronghold. As with the narrow boat and the minibus, it had been paid for with a credit card belonging to one of their non-military friends, so it was unlikely that it would be traced back to any of them. Their friend had been given the cash plus a little extra for his trouble, along with a family holiday that would end at the weekend, giving him the perfect reason for not informing the authorities about the purchases.

They planned to stop off in the nearby town to stock up on beer and snacks, and the local takeaways would be providing the catering that evening, but when they reached a point roughly a mile from the cottage, the minibus negotiated a bend and they found themselves confronted with a police roadblock a hundred yards ahead. The officers looked to be concentrating on cars coming from the opposite direction, but they couldn't take any chances.

'Heads up,' Levine said, and everyone craned to see what the problem was. Having identified the danger, the men in the back averted their gaze, not so much that they aroused suspicion, but enough to make identification a little harder. They had discussed the possibility of being stopped on the way and had decided that it wouldn't be the end of the world; they would go along quietly. All they had to do was hold out until seven thirty that evening, and after all the interrogation training they had been through, being questioned by plod didn't even come close to scary.

'Just chill, Barry, and act normally,' Levine said.

There were two police cars creating a chicane, with officers at either end allowing traffic to flow first in one direction, then the other. They followed the line of traffic as it crept towards the officer on point duty, Levine silently praying that they be allowed to pass unhindered.

It wasn't to be.

The armed officer raised his hand just as Barry was about to follow the car in front through the gap, then he signalled to his colleague at the other end of the roadblock to allow his stream of traffic to start moving.

'What do we do now?' Barry asked through clenched teeth, his gaze fixed ahead and his hands gripping the steering wheel in the ten-to-two position.

'First,' Levine said as jovially as possible, 'we drop the ventriloquist act. If you notice, they are only checking the cars coming from the other direction.'

Barry seemed to relax slightly as he saw that Levine was correct, but he was still ill at ease.

'What if they recognise us?'

'Why would they recognise you, Barry? Have you had your face plastered all over the front pages this week?'

'No, but I mean, the rest of you ... and how can you be so cool, like?'

'We've been in tighter spots than this,' Levine said, trying to keep a smile on his face despite the temptation to throw Barry through the windscreen. 'It's only a cop, for fuck's sake. It's not like the Sussex branch of Al-Qaeda just swarmed into view.'

The quip helped him loosen up a little, but he was still gripping the wheel tightly and staring at the officer, who was facing the other direction.

'Just a couple more minutes and we'll be through,' Levine said softly, doing his best to relax the driver, but Barry was having none of it. When the policeman turned to see how much traffic he was holding, he caught sight of Barry and knew instantly that something was amiss.

With a quick word into his radio, he approached the minibus, his right hand on the grip of the Heckler and Koch MP5 he was carrying, forefinger extended along the side of the trigger guard.

'Barry, chill, for fuck's sake,' Levine urged. 'Just answer his questions and we'll be on our way.'

The officer gestured for Barry to wind down the window, and he peered inside, taking in the scene.

'Is this your vehicle, sir?' Constable Stuart Fisher asked.

'Yes, Officer,' Barry said, and Levine could hear the tension in his voice. The policeman also sensed it, and the alarm bells started ringing.

'Turn the engine off and step out of the vehicle, please,' he said, and Barry turned to look at Levine, his eyes imploring him to do something. Carl simply nodded his head. 'Go on, then. Do as the officer says.'

Barry climbed out gingerly, and Levine knew the game was up when the driver raised his hands above his head in surrender.

The cop told Barry to assume the position up against the side of the bus, and he reached in and took the keys from the ignition, then told Levine to step down and move around the front of the vehicle, all the time keeping a watchful eye on him.

Another officer trotted up, having been summoned earlier, and he covered the two men while Fisher opened the back door and told everyone to get out. He stood back as they did so and immediately recognised three of the faces as they exited the vehicle.

'Lie face down on the ground and spread your arms and legs!' he shouted, all the time covering them with his weapon.

'Hotel Sierra, this is Tango Foxtrot Two Five.'

'Go ahead, Two Five.'

'I believe we have the eight suspects we're looking for in connection with the Tom Gray kidnappings.'

'Roger that; please hold.'

The other officer ordered Barry and Levine to the rear of the vehicle and instructed them to lie down next to their friends, then radioed the officers at the other end of the roadblock to bring up their handcuffs and some plasticuffs, temporary plastic binds used when no cuffs were available. Barry moaned at having to lie on the wet tarmac with the rain bouncing down all around him, but he got little sympathy.

Fisher read each of them their rights and all acknowledged him, except for Barry.

'I'm not one of them,' he pleaded. 'I'm just the driver. They hired me to bring them here.'

'He's telling the truth,' Levine said, glad of the opportunity to be rid of him, but Fisher was having none of it.

'Two Five, be advised, we have no available units at this time. You are requested to escort them to the command centre outside the old Sussex Renaissance Potteries building on the B3387.'

The officer recognised that as the location of the old pottery factory in which Tom Gray was holed up, and it wasn't very far away. The only problem was how to transport them. Two other armed officers ran over, and they began securing their suspects, and he used this time to come up with a plan of action.

His decision was to load them back into the minibus, and he climbed into the driver's seat while one of his colleagues sat in the back to keep an eye on the prisoners.

'Isn't this against health and safety regulations?' Paul Bennett asked whimsically. 'Shouldn't we have seatbelts or something?'

'Shut it,' the officer in the back chided. 'No talking.'

Ideally, Fisher would have kept the prisoners separated so that they couldn't formulate a defence against any upcoming charges, but without the manpower it was impossible. Besides, he thought, they had been hiding out together for a while now, which meant they had already had more than enough opportunity to get their stories straight. Couple that with the short journey time, and he didn't think it would make much of a difference.

Thankfully, none of them felt like talking, and they arrived at the outer perimeter within six minutes. Having radioed ahead, they were waved through the checkpoint and drove the last few hundred yards to the command vehicle, where they found Evan Davies waiting for them.

'Just leave them in the vehicle,' he told Fisher as he climbed out. 'Someone will be here shortly to pick them up.'

'Can you arrange transport to take us back to the roadblock?' the officer asked.

'No need. These guys will be transferred to another vehicle soon, and then you can take the minibus back.'

Davies looked through the windows and put names to faces for all of the passengers apart from Barry.

'Who's that?' he asked Fisher.

'Claims to be just the driver.'

'Let him go,' Davies said.

'Sir?'

'Release him,' Davies said, emphasising each syllable.

'But sir, he might be an accomplice. Shouldn't we at least—'

'We have our orders,' the superintendent broke in. 'Someone will be along in thirty minutes to collect the eight suspects. It's out of our hands now.'

'Do you want me to go down to the station with them? I am the arresting officer, after all.'

'I doubt they'll be going anywhere near a police station,' Davies told him. 'The orders came from the very top, so we just do as we're told. Get the driver out and stick him in the command vehicle for now. You can take him with you when you leave.'

Fisher did as instructed, but with a sense of betrayal: this was the biggest arrest of his career, and no one would hear about it. It probably wouldn't even be a factor when he came up for promotion, and that really pissed him off, and in turn he was a little aggressive as he dragged Barry from the back of the minibus.

Levine wasn't impressed with his manner. 'Take it easy,' he said. 'The guy's done nothing wrong. Wrong place at the wrong time, that's all.'

'Shut the fuck up,' Fisher snarled. 'You should be more concerned about your own safety.'

Levine snorted. 'I think we can handle a couple of hours in a police cell.'

'You should be so lucky,' Fisher said as he slammed the door closed.

'What's he talking about?' Levine asked.

'No idea,' the officer in the back of the van said. 'Just keep quiet.'

Harvey had watched the whole affair at the farmhouse on the video link provided by the helicopter and heard every word through his comms unit. When the confirmation came in that Sally was alive, he was relieved beyond measure and called the emergency services, just to be on the safe side.

'Ambulance on its way,' Harvey confirmed. 'I'm coming in.'

He gunned his motor, which resulted in him fishtailing around on the wet grass. He soon realised that slowly was going to be the quickest way out of the field, but once on the open road he floored the accelerator and was outside the farmhouse in no time.

Blythe was waiting at the back door by the time he arrived, having jogged in from the LUP. Harvey took off his comms gear and handed it back. 'Thanks.'

'Keep it,' Blythe said. 'You have comms to the police manning the roadblocks, and you can guide us in if they find anything. Meanwhile, we'll head back to our vehicles and wait to hear from you.'

'What about Gray? Is that assignment over?'

'It is for us. We would be unlikely to get the orders to take him down at this late stage, and the more pressing need is to find these terrorists. It's better to stay here, in the centre of the search area, so that we can deploy in any direction at a moment's notice.'

'That's good to hear,' Harvey said. 'Nice takedown, by the way. Was there no way of taking him alive, though?'

'I don't second-guess the squad leaders. If X-ray One had complied, he'd still be with us, but he made his choice, and we don't take any chances. At least he got a warning shout, and that is not something we do every day.'

Which is why they have built up such a fearsome reputation, Harvey thought.

He remembered the Balcombe Street siege in December 1975. Four suspected members of a provisional Irish Republican Army active service unit were chased through London after shooting through the windows of a Mayfair restaurant. This led to a six-day standoff in a block of flats, during which the four suspects held a married couple hostage. Negotiations were going nowhere, so knowing the suspects were following the events on the news, the authorities leaked information that the SAS had turned up to end the siege. The terrorists promptly freed the hostages and surrendered.

'I'll go and speak to Sally, see if she can give us a clue as to what Mansour is planning.'

He found her sitting on the couch, the bed sheet wrapped tightly around her, rocking gently back and forth.

The marks on her face looked superficial, but the real damage would be the psychological scars. She would get all the help she needed from the service, that was for sure, and eventually she would forget this episode, or at least learn to live with it. For now, though, he wanted her to recollect as much as possible.

'How are you holding up?' he asked her.

'I'm fine,' she said, but he could tell she was far from okay. Although she was looking at him, her focus was elsewhere.

'Sally, did they mention their target at any time?'

She shook her head. 'They spoke in Urdu, but used a few English words here and there. You know—words they don't have in their own language.'

'Which words? Do you remember any?'

'I heard "AK-47" a couple of times, but that's about it. They took me into a cellar somewhere but weren't with me for long—only about twenty minutes. After that it was Flynn ... '

Her voice tailed off as the recent memories came flooding back, but Harvey couldn't allow her to dwell, not just yet.

'What about Mansour? Did he speak to you?'

'Yes, he came in and told Flynn to leave, but he didn't say what his target was; he just wanted to know what I knew—what we knew—about him.'

Her eyes started to cloud over. 'I told him everything, everything I knew ... '

The tears came now, so he sat beside her and put a comforting arm around her shoulder.

'You did what you had to do,' he assured her. 'Most people would.'

The words didn't seem to comfort her, the tears still coming thick and fast.

'I doubt the information you gave him would do him any good,' he said. 'What exactly did you tell him?'

She managed to get herself under a semblance of control. 'I told him I was with the Service, and that we knew about his arrival.'

'That's it?'

Sally nodded.

'Then that's nothing he wouldn't have already guessed.' He ran his palm up and down her arm. 'It's okay, Sally. No one will blame you for any of this. We're all just so relieved that you're okay.'

She nodded again and blew her nose on the bed sheet.

'Are you sure Mansour didn't say anything at all about his target? How about the others?'

'Nothing, really. Well, there was one thing ... '

'What?'

'I'm sure it was nothing...'

Harvey wanted to shout at her to spit it out but knew that would be counterproductive. Instead he cajoled her gently.

'You never know, Sally. Even a single word could be significant.'

'Well, there were a few of them standing at the top of the cellar stairs, and I heard the word "grey" a few times. At first I thought they were probably talking about the weather, what with the sky being grey for the last few days, but later it occurred to me that it might be Tom Gray they were talking about.'

'Yes, we already made the connection,' Harvey said. 'We think the timing of his arrival in the UK was meant to take advantage of the fact that vast resources are being focused on the search for Gray's bomb.'

'No, not that, although it makes more sense, I guess...'

'If you have another theory, please share it,' Harvey said, even though he was sceptical of any ideas she might have.

'I was just thinking, maybe Gray is the target.'

Harvey thought about it, running through all possible connections between the two men but finding none. Gray had already left the army by the time Mansour came on the scene, and thinking back to both men's profiles, he was pretty sure that their paths hadn't crossed in recent years.

'I can't see any reason why he would target Gray,' he said. 'What would he gain?'

'At first I asked myself the same thing, but it boils down to one question: What would happen if Tom Gray were to die today? Think about it—why haven't we stormed the place yet?'

'Because,' he began, hoping to enlighten her, 'if we did, he would take his own life and the device he planted would...'

His voice tailed off as he made the connection. By killing Gray, Mansour would deprive them of all hope of finding his device. It was so simple, yet he hadn't even considered Gray as one of Mansour's possible targets; it was Sally who had actually figured it out.

Harvey put the SAS comms unit to his ear and was about to share his findings with Blythe, but the airwaves were already full of chatter, and he realised the revelation had come just too late.

Chapter Twenty-Four

Tom Gray was watching the BBC News channel, waiting to see if the home secretary would make his announcement on the justice bill before the second deadline passed. There was still an hour to go until the six o'clock target, but there was always the chance of an early press release, so he sat back to wait for it.

He'd checked on Stuart Boyle frequently, just to make sure he hadn't gone into shock. The last thing he wanted was the little shit dying on him. No, he wanted him to live a long time and remember this day for the rest of his life.

On his last visit to the cell, there had been no significant sign of internal bleeding, no signs of clammy skin or a fast but weak pulse, so he had left him to his crying. After checking that his other guests were still with him, he sat down for a final snack of Spam and potatoes, which he heated through on a Hexamine stove. Not the heartiest meal he'd ever prepared, he thought, and not really fitting the occasion, considering that this evening he would be celebrating in style with his friends.

And there was plenty to celebrate.

It had been a long week, with broken sleep and the constant feeling that the whole thing was about to go pear shaped, but in the end he'd achieved his goal: to get the country clamouring for a change in the law.

That he was able to exact his revenge on Stuart Boyle without recrimination was the cherry on the cake.

The original idea had been bandied about in the pub on the day of his wife's funeral, but no one had really taken the suggestion seriously.

However, the seed had been planted.

Over the coming days, as he'd put more and more thought into it, he'd realised that it might just be feasible, and he had got the guys together for a night in to see what their thoughts were. Naturally, some were sceptical at first, but as each obstacle was thrown in their path and they managed to find a way to overcome it, they parted that evening with a fledgling plan that developed quickly over the coming weeks.

There had been no doubt from the outset that they were taking a huge risk. Although a lot of things could be controlled, others relied on assumptions: that the world believed Simon Arkin was actually dead; that they would fall for the fake mines around his perimeter; that people believed he was willing to take his own life; that they would offer him the chance to face a single murder charge if he gave himself up.

That had been the biggest worry. If they hadn't come up with that offer, he would be facing life in prison with no chance of parole. Even if he did manage to get released, he would be a very old man by the time he got out. His friends, many with families, faced a similar fate if that part hadn't come off, but when Olemwu's father called him a coward, it gave him the opportunity he was looking for. Of course, there was no way of knowing that Vincent Olemwu would make that remark, but there had been four other ways they could have steered the security service around to offering that deal, all of which were superfluous now. One had been to make sure his eight friends were implicated, and all that took was to contact them frequently in the days leading up to the first webcast. To be doubly sure, they'd picked up a couple of the boys when they were with friends, so that they would be able to identify them. Gray guessed the security services would try to use emotional blackmail, and giving them the ammunition had been easy.

At first he'd insisted that he carry out the whole thing himself, as he really had felt he had nothing to lose, and he hadn't wanted his friends giving up their liberty. Sure, he'd wanted to create a trail to the others, but they would all have watertight alibis when they eventually handed themselves in. His friends had understood his reasons but had insisted on taking part. Besides, Campbell had argued, the only way they could truly be implicated was if they were seen to take part in the abductions. He'd reluctantly agreed, but on the condition that they each took a hundred grand in cash and stashed it away in case the excrement hit the twirly wind machine.

He smiled as he thought of the justice bill that the country had voted overwhelmingly to support. The suggestion that the whole country get a say in whether the law was changed to come down harder on repeat offenders had been a touch of genius on Michael Fletcher's part. Originally it was to have been Tom who would demand a review of the current system, but putting the vote to the people had been an inspired idea. The decision from the government on the future referendum might not be in yet, but something would be done, he was sure of it. The opposition party was already jumping on the bandwagon, but whether they kept their word if they came to power remained to be seen. One thing was for sure: if they made a promise and went back on it, the country would never forgive them.

His favourite part of the new bill was the reintroduction of National Service, though he wasn't too sure the birch was such a good idea. It certainly hadn't had much effect on Joseph Olemwu, apart from making him an even angrier young man. Even now, a day after administering the punishment, Olemwu had still been defiant when he'd visited his cell.

No matter, he lived the gang culture and that would seal his fate in the not-so-distant future. Another black youth stabbed or shot in the streets, and barely a handful of people would give a shit.

All he had to do now was to make a final webcast accepting the home secretary's offer, and he would walk out the door. There was always the chance that the public wouldn't vote for him to surrender himself, but one click of the mouse had activated a command on his South African server which had disregarded all incoming emails and instead sent back the results showing that the people wanted him to give himself up. Moments after he left the building, the police would enter and find Simon Arkin alive and well, and the sole charge he was facing would be dropped, making him a free man.

They would certainly be surprised that Arkin had survived his 'execution', when in fact all it had taken was a blood pack and a blank round. The trickiest part had been to get the struggling boy to slump when the shot was fired, and this had been achieved by having a drip attached to his right arm, hidden under the long sleeve of his T-shirt. The drip was activated by a button that he'd taped to the wall right next to the light switch, and as he'd entered the room he'd hit the button a couple of times, administering a dose large enough to render him unconscious but not large enough to kill him.

Wouldn't that have been ironic: faking the boy's death and actually murdering him in the process! Fortunately he had an ex-colleague who now worked as an anaesthetist at a large hospital, and getting just the right amount of Propofol to knock him out for a couple of minutes hadn't been a problem.

He'd stood in the doorway, blocking the camera's view until the boy was under, then fired the 'fatal' shot before going to complete the illusion by checking his pulse.

The final part of the plan was to give the authorities a big enough reason not to launch a rescue mission, and so one of his last acts as the managing director of Viking Security Services had been to use his connections to arrange a free security appraisal of Norden Industries. The purpose was not to actually take anything, but to come up with a feasible scenario that would convince them that he actually had a weapon. The one he'd come up with would have kept them occupied for a few weeks, never mind just the few days he needed.

One concern was that any agreement they made would be conditional on him giving the location of the device, so he'd really created one which would take thousands of lives, with the emphasis on 'small' and 'airborne'. They'd not be best pleased when they discovered that it was a small incendiary device hidden under a beehive in a nearby apiary. If it went off, thousands of lives would indeed be lost: the lives of thousands of small, airborne insects. He'd been careful never to say that thousands of *people* would die, so technically he had told the truth. If they had chosen to interpret his words differently, that was their problem.

Had it all been worth it?

It had been a gamble, that was for sure, and some might have argued that if he'd simply beaten the shit out of Boyle, he would have probably got a few months inside, maybe a suspended sentence because of the mitigating circumstances. However, he had wanted to punish Boyle *and* do something about the judicial system. When the judge had allowed Boyle to get away with eight months on remand after depriving Gray of a family, he had seen that as a huge slap in the face. Crippling the boy and walking away scot-free was going to be the perfect 'fuck you' to Justice A. B. Benson.

Even if his justice bill never saw the light of day, he hoped this last week would at least let the government know that soft sentences were not palatable and that people would no longer accept them.

As he polished off the last of the Spam, he thought about how pissed off Andrew Harvey would be. He'd really given him the run around; having him search the country for a device he would never find; leaving a trail to his friends, one that Harvey wouldn't be able to follow to its conclusion; and getting Harvey to come all the way down here just to deliver a document.

When Harvey found out that this really *was* mostly about revenge, he wasn't going to be adding him to his Christmas card list, but hurting a spook's feelings wasn't going to cause him to lose sleep.

He sat back in his chair, looking forward to a few beers later and satisfied that he'd thought of everything.

Everything apart from the fucking smell.

As Abdul Mansour approached the line of media vans along the side of the road, he was glad to see that the two lead cars and the pair of motorcycles were already parked in their designated positions.

So far, the journey from the farm had been without incident, and as planned, he was bringing up the rear of their little convoy. They had followed his instructions and kept other cars between them up until the last couple of miles, but as traffic thinned out, they found they were the only vehicles on the road. No matter, they had reached their destination, and in moments he would be firing the first shot in what he hoped would be his greatest victory so far. Hoped, because no matter how good the tactics, no matter how good the planning, there was always the unexpected.

Admittedly, they'd only had a day to practise their attack, but even if they'd had a month, there would still be countless obstacles waiting to trip them up: An over-zealous policeman could have stopped a car for having a taillight out; a pedestrian could have walked in front of one of their cars; police reinforcements could have been brought in to contain the crowds for when Gray turned himself in, resulting in a greater opposing force; the RPGs might not work; the motorbikes might...

There wasn't time to dwell on what might or might not happen.

Another car pulled into position at the head of the news vans, the occupants remaining inside, awaiting his signal. They received cursory glances from the media folk, but nothing more.

He was seventy yards from his destination now, and the first of his vehicles was rolling to a stop.

It was all in Allah's hands now.

Sixty yards from his intended position, and it seemed Allah wasn't in the best of moods.

No sooner had the first car stopped than a policeman approached, an MP5 held across his midriff. He got to within ten yards of the vehicle when the occupants leapt out and began spraying hot metal in his general direction.

Damn them!

He specifically told them not to open fire until he had given the signal, which was firing off the first RPG round, and he definitely instructed them not to select automatic fire!

Their bullets were flying high and wide of the mark, while the officer returned fire more accurately, laying down single rounds as he retreated hastily. Within seconds he was being covered by two of his colleagues who were crouching behind their vehicle, and two of Mansour's men went down in quick succession. Another had expended his entire magazine within a few seconds and was struggling to get a replacement from his jacket pocket when two rounds caught him in the chest, and another threw up a crimson spray from the back of his head as he fell.

The attack was falling apart before it had even started, and the police were quickly gaining the upper hand. The two remaining cars had stopped dead, leaving him twenty yards farther away than he would ideally have liked, but still well within range of the police cars.

'Everyone out now!' he shouted. 'Lay down fire while I get into position!'

All four men in the car jumped out of the passenger side doors, keeping the vehicle between themselves and the incoming fire. As the other three added to the volley of fire being directed towards the police cars, he slung the first of the two RPGs onto his shoulder, raised the rear sight to manually cock the weapon and took careful aim.

Perhaps Allah was looking out for him after all, he thought, as the angle he was forced to fire from exposed the rear of the first police vehicle, which wouldn't have been the case if he had stopped where he'd originally planned.

Despite the staccato buzz of gunfire all around him, he took a breath and exhaled slowly before pressing the trigger. The high explosive anti-tank, or HEAT, round, found its mark, penetrating the side panel of the Volvo before detonating a millisecond later over the petrol tank. The force of the explosion threw the car four feet into the air, and the policemen taking refuge behind it were flattened by the overpressure, the lightning-fast shockwave literally crushing their internal organs.

The driver of the other vehicle was calling in the attack to his superiors when the grenade hit, but his report was cut short as searing hot shards of shrapnel shredded the vehicle, a piece of the rear wheel arch removing the top half of his head.

'Move to your positions!' Mansour shouted. 'You lot, make sure they're all dead, then attack the command vehicle. The rest of you, come with me.'

A bullet flew past his ear, and he ducked instinctively. It had come from the direction of the field, and he realised that the armed officers surrounding the building had run over to investigate the initial explosion and were looking to exact revenge for the deaths of their colleagues.

Mansour reached into the car, grabbed the other RPG and slung it over his shoulder, then grabbed his AK-47 and began putting rounds down to suppress the incoming barrage. His first shot missed by a hair's breadth, but the second found its mark, the policeman crumpling to the ground clutching his stomach.

His men had already begun the process of rounding up the reporters and their technicians, and were herding them all towards the middle media van. Through a gap in the hedge, he saw that the six men lying at the ridge were already engaging their targets, and he instructed five of his men to leave the reporters to the others and take positions at the hedge, to help keep the police under pressure.

His men were now attacking from three sides, and he saw two more of the enemy go down, but at the cost of six more of his own people.

All he had to do now was keep the enemy totally pinned down and let Zulfir destroy the door to the building. Once he'd done that, it would be time to signal the riders.

———

At the sound of the first gunshots, all eight men turned as best they could to look through the rear windows of the minibus, but with their hands cuffed behind their backs, it was no mean feat. Their view was also obscured by the policemen, who were peering down the road to where the battle was now raging.

'What the fuck's going on?' Paul Bennett asked, a touch of concern in his voice. It wasn't the thought of being present when the bullets were flying; it was being present when the bullets were flying while being trussed up like a turkey and unable to defend himself that bothered him.

'I don't know,' their guard said, opening the back door to go and investigate.

'Wait!' Levine said. 'That's gunfire, and it sounds like AK-47s. They aren't police issue. You have to let us go, now.'

'Just wait here, I'll see what's going on.'

'We can help—trust me,' Levine persisted.

'Look, there's no way I'm letting you go. Just sit tight, I'll be—'

Over five hundred yards away, Parwan Chaudhury flew backwards, the 9mm round from the police MP5 catching him five inches below the chin and travelling through his body to decimate his spine. As he fell, he was completely unaware that the penultimate bullet he'd fired had missed its intended target but had found another place to land. The bullet travelled far beyond the maximum effective range of the AK-47, but as it hit the officer's right eye, it had enough momentum to pass through and lodge in the soft tissue of his brain.

Their guard fell backwards into the aisle of the minibus, blood pouring from the eye socket. Paul Bennett's training kicked in, and from the rear seat he quickly manoeuvred himself over the body and fell onto it, fumbling blindly around the dead officer's waist for his handcuff keys. Another bullet slammed into the rear door of the bus as he groped around the belt, and he took it as a sign to get his arse in gear.

Colin Avery also offered some gentle encouragement.

'Get a fucking move on, Bennett!'

Bennett eventually located the key but found it tricky to insert it into the lock, the rigid steel bar of the Hiatt handcuffs hampering his efforts. It took three attempts, during which he dropped the key twice, before he managed to unlock one of the cuffs. Quickly removing the other, he in turn released Colin Avery and handed him the key, then grabbed the MP5 and a spare magazine from the dead man's belt.

As he opened the rear door and jumped out, he saw and then heard the explosion at the other end of the lane.

Avery jumped down beside him. 'Just like the good old days,' he said. 'But I think we're going to need a lot more than one weapon between the eight of us.'

'Then let's go ask the nice policeman,' Bennett suggested, and they sprinted over to the command vehicle. Bennett was first up the stairs, and as Fisher opened the door to see the source of the explosion, Bennett pushed him to the floor and burst into the cramped vehicle, with Avery following close behind.

'Knock, knock,' Avery said.

Davies was busy informing his superiors about the attack, and when the two prisoners rushed in brandishing the machine pistol, he thought his time had come. He raised his hands slowly, as did Fisher, who still lying on his back.

'Don't shoot,' Davies said. 'Just go with your friends. No one else needs to die.'

Bennett was confused for a moment; then the realisation dawned. 'You think these people have come to rescue us?'

Davies nodded. 'Obviously. Why else would they be attacking us?'

'We don't need to be rescued,' Bennett pointed out. 'We'll be walking free in a couple of hours.'

'Then who are they after?' Fisher asked.

Avery offered a hand and helped him to his feet. 'I don't know,' he said, 'but we have to stop them.'

'What have you done to Bainbridge?' Fisher asked.

'Who's Bainbridge?'

'He was with you in the bus,' he said. 'How did you get his weapon?'

'Bainbridge is down,' Avery said without emotion. 'They shot him. Speaking of weapons, what have you got in your arsenal?'

Davies used his head to gesture towards a cabinet on his right.

'Put your hands down,' Bennett said, 'we're on the same side.'

Davies did as he was told and opened the gun cabinet. 'We have three more MP5s and four Glocks,' he said, studying the contents.

'We'll take them all.' Avery took off his jacket and laid it on the counter, then grabbed the weapons and ammunition and placed them on top, before bundling it up.

'I'll distribute these,' he said, lugging the makeshift holdall out of the door.

'I assume you've called in backup,' Bennett said to Davies, and the superintendent nodded.

'Good. When they get here, let them know we're the good guys,' and he ran out to join the others.

Barry had been sitting in the back of the command vehicle throughout, not saying a word, just taking in the surreal scene. He had been thinking about how he could incorporate Levine's Afghan heroics into his book, but now he was about to witness firsthand the SAS in action, and it would give him an ending that would put any previous fictional work to shame. All he had to do was live through it...

When Gray heard the faint sound of the first gunshot, he dismissed it, but when it was followed up by the distinctive Clack! Clack! Clack! of an AK-47 on automatic fire, and his motion sensors suddenly went berserk, he switched his attention to the monitors. The sensors were being tripped by the armed police running to the southern corner of the field, so he switched to the camera covering that sector just in time to see two men in the lane fall to the ground.

He could see at least twenty people firing towards the two police cars, and his immediate thought was that they were complete amateurs. They stood like the hero in an action movie, rather than shooting from cover, and they were wasting ammunition at an astonishing rate. As the third man fell, he caught sight of the man at the rear of the line of cars firing the RPG, destroying the police vehicles.

The attackers split up, some heading up the lane towards the command vehicle, the others towards the media vans. He saw a policeman collapse in the field, and panning his camera to the left, he saw that there were people on the ridge two hundred yards from the building. He was flanked on three sides now, and that only meant one thing: he was their target.

Why, he had no idea, and there wasn't time to worry about it. All that mattered for the moment was repelling their attack. If only he'd brought more weapons than the 9mm Browning and the ancient ex-army issue L1A1 self-loading rifle, he'd have half a chance, but he only had a magazine of ammunition for each. He figured that if he had to use them, it would be to warn anyone approaching the building rather than for full-blown defence.

He removed the Browning magazine containing the blanks and inserted one containing thirteen live rounds, then loaded the SLR with a twenty-round mag and ran up the stairs to the window affording him a view of the hostiles on the ridge. They currently presented the greatest danger to the police officers in the field and had to be taken out first.

Gray removed the bottom board from the window and stuck the barrel of the SLR through the gap. His first round fell short, so he adjusted his aim slightly and squeezed the trigger again, this time hitting the attacker in the shoulder. Not a kill shot, but it put the man out of action, and Gray moved on to the next target. His next shot was a clean kill, but he had drawn attention to himself, and rounds began to pepper the boards around his head. He ducked to the left, restricting his field of fire but still giving him a shot at two of the hostiles at the far end of the ridge.

Although this firing position reduced his visible profile, it also meant he couldn't see Zulfir at the other end of the ridge, preparing his RPG and taking aim at the main door of the building.

The HEAT round hit high, punching a hole in the wall above the door and projecting debris throughout the interior. A breeze block the size of a loaf of bread smashed into the computer table, destroying his laptop and ricocheting into the bank of monitors, while other smaller fragments of concrete shrapnel fizzed around the room. A splinter buried itself in Gray's buttock, stinging like a hornet, and he fell to the floor, the concussion from the explosion disorientating him momentarily.

He shook his head and opened his mouth wide to equalise the pressure, then pushed himself up and surveyed the damage. His equipment had been decimated, but the generator was still going, though all it had to feed now was the lights.

The round had come from the ridge—of that he was sure—and when he returned to the window, he saw his assailant preparing to take another shot, the weapon already poised on his shoulder. Grabbing the rifle, he took a snap shot, but the bullet went wide. His next effort went high, but the third smashed into the man's forehead, throwing him backwards, but not before the grenade left the tube.

Gray threw himself to the floor and covered his ears as the projectile arched towards the building, finding its mark and demolishing the front door.

As the sound of the explosion died down, Gray heard two long blasts on a whistle coming from the right, and he identified the person responsible as the one who'd fired the first RPG at the police. This was undoubtedly the leader and therefore his priority target.

Priority, that was, until he saw the motorcycles enter the field behind the ridge. The riders raced towards the rising ground and swept over the crest, making a beeline for the path leading to his door.

There was now no doubt in Tom Gray's mind that he was the intended target, and it seemed that the men on the bikes were intent on finishing him off at close range. He checked the inner wall and was glad to see that it remained intact, although there were signs of damage, a large circle of bricks protruding outwards like a huge blister. It wouldn't take much more to breach it, so the men on the bikes had to be stopped before they got close enough to try. As he raised his rifle again and took aim, he saw the biker in the black jacket slump forward onto the handlebars, and the bike skewed from side to side before tossing the rider and settling on the sodden ground.

A glance to his left and he saw three figures in civvies running into the field, MP5s raised and pouring lead ahead of their advance.

Gray squinted as he thought he recognised them.

Bennett?

Avery?

Fletcher?

What the hell were they doing here?

The sight of his friends rushing towards the ridge had caught him totally by surprise, and he'd almost forgotten about the other rider, who was powering onwards and only twenty yards from the door. He raised the rifle and snapped off a few rounds, and while some missed, others pinged off the bike in a shower of sparks but failed to do any significant damage. The rider was also in his friends' sights, but Nadeem was wiser than Kamran, and he played the throttle, first speeding up, then braking before instantly applying the gas again, just as Mahmood had shown him. Mahmood had said this would make it harder for anyone firing at him to get a proper lead. Nadeem had no idea what that meant, so Mahmood had explained that when aiming at a moving target, you had to fire in front of it so that the target and bullet arrived at the same point at the same time. If the target were moving at a constant speed, this could become quite easy with practise, but by speeding up and slowing down, it made the shooter's task much more difficult.

It certainly worked for Nadeem, and he made it to the entrance. However, once the bike had stopped, he became a sitting duck for the experienced soldiers and took several rounds in the back as he hurdled over the debris that had once been the front door to the building. The impact punched him up against the inner wall, and he collapsed in a heap, his left hand millimetres from the trigger for his vest.

Mansour was standing in a gap between two media vans when he saw Nadeem go down, and was proud that he'd managed to get as close as he had.

Allah would truly reward him.

Digging the mobile from his pocket, he thumbed through the contacts list, selected 'Red' from the list and hit the 'Call' button.

Nothing happened.

Wait a moment...

Still nothing.

Incredulous, he was checking that he had a signal when the explosion came, shaking the ground beneath him. The shockwave shoved him backwards, but he just about managed to keep his feet. The hedges surrounding the field were buffeted, and satellite dishes were blown from the roofs of the media vehicles, and he saw that everyone else on the battlefield was stunned into inaction by the violence of the blast.

As the dust settled, he saw that the building had sustained a huge amount of damage. A hole the size of a bus had been blown out of the front wall; part of the roof had collapsed at the rear corner; and the majority of the boards covering the windows on the upper floor had been blown out. It was hard to imagine anyone inside surviving the explosion, certainly not anyone near the blast point.

While everyone was recovering from the impact of the blast, Mansour ran past the media vans and jumped into one of the cars, performed a neat three-point turn and sped off down the lane towards the nearest village. He had said that he would signal with several short blasts of his whistle when it was time to retreat, but he needed time to make good his escape, and his men, Allah praise them, would provide him with it, keeping the enemy at bay and preventing them from pursuing him.

He knew there would be roadblocks all around the area, but that didn't concern him. All he needed to do was reach the village and make a couple of phone calls.

Gray watched the rider disappear beneath him and lost the shot, but when he saw his friends offer a couple of double-taps each, then move on, he knew the X-ray was dead. He turned his attention back to the leader and saw him standing next to the rear door of a Sky News van, and he swung the rifle round, taking aim.

He's certainly a cool customer, Gray thought as he watched the man standing in the midst of a battle and still finding time to make a phone call, but he was about to cancel the guy's tariff permanently.

He had a bead on the target and was increasing the pressure on the trigger, when his world collapsed.

The explosion was like nothing he'd ever experienced. His head seemed to contract, and he felt a free-falling sensation as the gantry on which he was kneeling disappeared beneath him. Everything became silent and the drop happened in slow motion, tumbling downwards into the grey mist of brick dust thrown out by the blast. He thrust an arm out in a feeble attempt to grab at the ceiling, but it slowly receded before being consumed by the cloud of debris.

He fell for what seemed an eternity, as if the floor no longer existed and instead he was making the journey straight to hell, spiralling downwards relentlessly.

He didn't feel the moment of impact.

There was light, streaming in through the hole that suddenly appeared in the roof. Then an instant later there was just darkness.

Jeff Campbell and Tristram Barker-Fink were through the gaping hole before the dust even settled, while Sonny Baines, Len Smart and Carl Levine rushed to see to Bennett and the other two who had led the counterattack.

They each tended to one of their friends, but Sonny soon felt a hand on his shoulder.

'Fletch is gone,' Smart said, and moved on to inform Levine. Sonny took the news stoically, simply nodded and turned his attention back to Avery and his injuries. Blood was seeping from his ears and his left leg was bent up underneath him, and Sonny was grateful that he was unconscious.

'We need medics,' he shouted over to Levine.

'No chance. They aren't going to send an ambulance crew into the middle of a battle.'

'Fair enough,' Sonny said, grabbing Avery's weapon and the spare magazines. 'Let's go end it.'

He ran to his left, and Smart and Levine followed him as he reached the top of the ridge, level with the two remaining attackers. The six pounds of metal in his hands spat twice, and the nearest hostile lay motionless. Beyond him the other target appeared, raising himself to his knees as he swung his AK-47 round. The movement was all too slow, and he was pushed backwards by the force of the impact, both bullets catching him in the sternum.

With the ridge clear, the three men spread out and headed towards the hedge marking the boundary of the field. Incoming rounds peppered the ground around them, but the intensity dropped as, one by one, the attackers exhausted their meagre supply of ammunition.

Sonny saw four men pile into a car and shoot off in the opposite direction from the burning wreckage of the police vehicles, and he chased them with a couple of short bursts from the MP5. The rounds shattered the back windscreen, but the driver kept his foot on the gas, screaming round the corner out of sight. Sonny had no way of knowing if he'd manage to hit anyone, but it didn't matter, because a bullet flashed just over his head to remind him that there were still plenty of hostiles remaining.

The incoming rounds were coming from the lane leading up to the command vehicle, so he laid down some covering fire while Smart and Levine advanced, firing as they moved. When they dropped to a kneeling position and continued to pepper the hedge with accurate fire, Sonny ran past them and took out one of the hostiles with a head shot. Two more shots came his way, and then he saw the remaining two shooters jump up and run towards the burning vehicles, their empty weapons discarded by the roadside. As far as Sonny was concerned, an unarmed foe was simply a foe capable of arming himself again, so he had no qualms about giving them both the good news in the back.

The only remaining opposition came from the direction of the media vans, and Sonny burst through the hedge and approached from the lane, swiftly changing out his magazine as he moved, the weapon sweeping from side to side as he searched for his next kill. Levine and Smart were at his six, and they spread out across the road, advancing slowly.

A figure ran out from between two vans and stopped dead, surprise written all over his face. The AK-47 in his right hand clattered to the ground and he raised his hands, but didn't find anyone in the mood for taking prisoners. With one friend dead, two more seriously injured and Tom Gray unaccounted for, the three men didn't even have to exchange glances to know what the others were thinking. Each fired a double-tap, and the enemy headcount decreased by one more.

Smart went left, Levine and Sonny to the right, and they moved slowly but with purpose down the line of vehicles. They cleared past two before they encountered and dispatched another hostile, then came towards the larger vehicle near the middle of the queue. The rear door was open, and Smart could see people packed inside like sardines, and as he reached the edge of the preceding van, he understood why they looked terrified.

'Drop it!'

The command came from a boy barely eighteen, his AK-47 trained on the hostages. Smart saw his two mates approaching the kid from the rear and did as he was ordered, hoping to attract his fire. The plan worked and the youngster swung the rifle towards him, but didn't even get close to getting Len in his sights, the front of his face blowing outwards before he clattered to the floor.

Smart indicated for the people to remain in the van and kept guard as the other two continued to clear each vehicle in turn, but when they returned three minutes later, he gestured for everyone to climb down one at a time, all three men keeping a keen eye out for any possible hostiles squirreled among them.

Once the area was secure, Sonny jogged back to the command vehicle and instructed them to call in the paramedics, then trotted over to the building to see what had become of Tom. Policemen were already tending to the wounded, including Bennett and Avery, making them comfortable until the ambulances arrived.

He climbed over the rubble to where Campbell, Levine, Smart and Barker-Fink were tossing debris to one side.

'Where's Tom?' he asked.

'Under this lot,' Campbell said. 'Give us a hand.'

Sonny scrambled over to them and saw a finger poking out from the side of the debris, and he joined them in tossing half bricks and wooden stakes towards the side of the room. It was a couple of moments before he realised that only three of the prisoners' cells remained standing, the two closest to the front door having been completely demolished. No sound was coming from any of the remaining cells, but he wasn't going to lose sleep over it.

All he cared about was getting Tom out.

They continued the excavation for another couple of minutes, until finally Gray's head and chest were clear, and neither looked particularly pretty. His entire head was purple and swollen, and his right cheek had been sliced open, revealing the jawbone beneath. His chest was a mass of blood, and Levine fought in vain to find a pulse.

Campbell pushed him aside and began to administer CPR, but Sonny backed off, knowing it was far too late.

As he clambered towards the entrance, he saw the rain had stopped, and a thin ray of sunlight forced its way through a hole in the clouds, but nothing was going to brighten up his day.

The scene around him was chaotic. Some of the media people in the lane were howling and comforting each other, while others had grabbed cameras and were filming all they could, no gory scene left unrecorded. One tried to make his way through the hole in the building, but Sonny grabbed him by the collar and swung him round before smashing his nose with his forehead.

The cameraman collapsed in a heap, clutching his face and trying to stem the flow of blood.

'Fucking parasite,' Sonny spat. 'You want to be on my battlefield, you carry a rifle, not a fucking camera.'

He kicked out at the figure on the floor, who took the hint and scuttled away, leaving a hundred thousand pounds worth of video equipment lying on the ground.

The sound of sirens in the distance shook Sonny from his rage, and he went to see how the living were getting on, starting with Bennett.

Chapter Twenty-Five

'Emergency, what service do you require?'

'Ambulance! My aunt has collapsed and isn't breathing. She's seventy years old.'

'What is your address?'

Mansour read out the details from a gas bill on the table. 'Please, come quickly!'

'Okay, someone will be with you in seven minutes. In the meantime, have you administered CPR before?'

'No, but my brother has. He's doing it now,' Mansour said, and pretended to pass further instructions to his nonexistent sibling. He was actually sitting in the lounge of the cottage, which he'd chosen the night before as he'd reconnoitred the area. He'd selected it because it was isolated, and he could park his vehicle behind it, away from prying eyes. The old lady on the floor may well have been someone's aunt, but it wasn't a heart attack she was suffering from; it was severe blood loss caused by the gaping wound in her throat.

While he waited for the ambulance to arrive, he put the corner of a tablecloth over his handset and dialled the pay-as-you-go mobile phone he had purchased at the airport and given to the imam, Amir Channa, at the mosque.

'Brother, I have finished work and need a lift home,' he said. He knew full well that GCHQ would be listening to all calls coming from the immediate area—or at least he expected them to be—hence the reason for disguising his voice and using code.

'Okay' was the simple reply, and that told Mansour that the prearranged pick-up was still on. The imam would now give the sim card from the phone to one of his trusted followers and have him take it on a bus ride and drop it into someone's bag, leading the authorities far from the mosque should the phone call ever be flagged up. The phone itself would be tossed into a garbage bin, ready to be taken away and crushed.

He sat back in the chair and took the chance to reflect on the past few days. That his idea had been accepted by the elders was an achievement in itself, but to carry it out with so little notice and under the watchful eyes of the world's media was bound to elevate his status. The audacity of the raid would become the stuff of legend, and his name would become known and feared throughout the western world.

Of course, he regretted the fact that many of his men had died and that the rest would surely be captured, but they had served Allah well, and their rewards would be waiting for them in *Jannah*.

He stood and went to the window, glad to see that the rain had finally stopped and the clouds were dispersing. It was as if Allah had sent the downpour to help him complete the mission, and now that it was over, He was showing His gratitude with the beautiful rainbow on the horizon.

While he was appreciating the natural phenomenon, he caught sight of the ambulance approaching in the distance, and he stepped through the front door and waited at the garden gate, waving his arms frantically as it approached. The vehicle pulled up, and both the driver and passenger got out and headed to the rear to get their AED, the automated external defibrillator, from the back. Mansour followed them and climbed in, the pistol already in his hand. The driver sensed him climbing in and was about to tell him to get out, when the barrel of the gun was pointed in his face.

'Do as I ask and you might live,' Mansour said calmly.

The paramedics dropped their equipment and raised their hands.

'We have to deal with an emergency,' the female said, her voice quivering.

'Sadly, you are too late to save the old lady,' he said. 'Now, can you both drive this thing?'

The couple nodded, the woman close to losing control but the man holding it together better.

'You,' Mansour said, pointing to the male, 'take her coat off and strap her into the stretcher, nice and tight.'

The female paramedic almost fainted when he gave his instructions and had to be helped onto the bed by her colleague, who uttered soft words in an attempt to soothe her.

With the female secured, he ordered the man to climb through the small gap into the driver's seat. Then he put on the woman's high-visibility jacket. It was a snug fit but would help with the illusion, and he completed the look with a disposable cap and surgical mask.

'What is your name?' Mansour asked.

'John.'

'Drive, John,' he said, 'and turn on the siren.'

The medic did as he was told, and Mansour took a seat on the free stretcher, his gun trained on the driver.

'Where are we going?'

'South,' Mansour told him. 'Head for the A23, then join the A27 westbound towards Worthing. There will be police roadblocks on the way, but I want to go through them. Use whatever excuse you need, but if you reveal my presence, the first bullet will be yours, and your friend will be next.'

He searched around inside a box and found some tape and a bandage which he used to cover the woman's mouth. He felt sure the man would obey instructions, but this female was such a wreck, she might start screaming at any moment.

Sure enough, not ten minutes into the journey, as they approached the dual carriageway, they came across the first police checkpoint. Traffic was backed up three hundred yards, and John asked what to do next.

'Do what you would normally do,' Mansour said, exasperated. 'Use the other lane, get to the head of the queue and drive through.'

Oncoming traffic pulled over as the driver rushed towards the police cars, and John frantically thought of a way to let the police know he was in trouble. Sadly for him, and to Mansour's great relief, the police manning the point ushered him through, and they continued onto the A23, southbound towards Brighton.

'Good, good,' Mansour said, more to himself than the driver.

Traffic was heavy, but the blues and twos soon shifted anything in front of them, and soon they reached the outskirts of Brighton and turned onto the A27.

'There is a lay-by just after the tunnel ahead, and a black Volvo should be waiting. Pull in behind it.'

The small parking area appeared three miles along the road, and the car was indeed parked up. The paramedic pulled in and stopped close to the back of it, and Mansour told him to silence the siren.

'Get in here,' he said, and gestured for John to climb through the gap.

'Lie down.'

The man did so, and Mansour quickly strapped him into the other stretcher, then searched his pockets and found his wallet.

'Nice family,' he said, examining a photo. 'It would be a shame for anything to happen to them, which is why I suggest you lie still until someone arrives to free you. If I am followed today, I will know it was you who told them where I was, and my followers will exact my revenge.'

He took John's driver's licence from the wallet and stuffed it into his trousers. 'I now know where you live, John, so lie down and wait to be rescued. When that time comes, tell them that Abdul Mansour will be back one day, and they should tremble at the thought.'

With that, he jumped out of the ambulance and into the waiting car, which sped off towards Shoreham airport and the waiting Cessna which would fly him first to a small airport outside of Paris, then on to Tirana in Albania, where he would take a different mode of transport home.

His threat to return was an empty one, and he knew it. His profile would be raised to a whole new level internationally, and it would be almost impossible to get into the West again after this, but in the months and years to come they would be expecting another attack, and that would only enhance his reputation and compound their fear.

He would only relax completely once he was back home in Quetta, but for now he closed his eyes and savoured the victory a little more.

Epilogue

He woke and immediately felt confused. It took some time for his brain to kick into gear, but even then he could only focus on objects, not take in any detail. He stared at the ceiling fan above his head, humming gently as it spun slowly. He saw it, but it didn't register as a fan, just movement, hypnotic and calming.

Movement from the corner of his eye broke the spell, and a man appeared next to him. The man was talking, but he didn't hear the words, just saw the lips moving. As quickly as he'd appeared, the man was gone again, leaving him to stare at the fan some more.

Sleep, his body said.

He desperately wanted his head to clear, but putting a thought together was like trying to swim through treacle. He wanted to remember something, anything, but all he could concentrate on was the fan, mesmerising, round and round and round . . .

Sleep.

He closed his eyes to help his concentration levels, but nothing came, just an image of the fan, turning relentlessly.

Then sleep.

When he opened his eyes again, the room was darker, the afternoon sun giving way to twilight. The fan was still there, and the man had returned. No, not the same man. This one was taller, different hair, white complexion, not olive-skinned like the other.

He realised that his ability to think had returned and immediately searched for answers inside the fog that was his memory.

Nothing.

The man stood over him, arms behind his back.

'Good morning, Tom,' he said, his accent suggesting public school and privilege.

'Where—'

The word had barely escaped his lips when the pain from his jaw shot to the top of his skull. He winced, then tried again, gently this time.

'Where am I?'

'My, how original,' the man said. 'I must say, I expected more from you.'

He introduced himself as James Farrar and had an air of condescension about him: Gray took an immediate dislike to the man.

Tom repeated his question despite the pain it caused.

'Subic,' Farrar replied.

Gray searched his memory for the name, and it came after a moment.

'Manila?'

'Close. The nearest town is actually Olongapo, but Manila isn't that far away. Couple of hours in a decent vehicle, if you can find one in this God-forsaken country.'

'How—'

'Tom, you really are disappointing me. "Where am I? How did I get here? What do you want from me?" At least you seem to know your own name, which is a start I suppose. Well, let me save you some time.

'The "where", as I already mentioned, is Subic Bay Freeport. Our colonial friends left in 1991, and the locals turned it into a thriving business area, but the Americans retained a small interest, including this house. It was once the billet of an admiral, you know.'

Gray was unimpressed. He didn't care if Lord Nelson himself had slept in the very same bed; he just wanted answers.

'The "how" was a Hercules transport plane which picked you up from Farnborough all those weeks ago. The—'

'Wait. What do you mean, all those weeks ago? How long have I been here?'

'Almost two months now. I must say, you really were a mess when you arrived, and I wouldn't trust the local medical staff as far as I could throw them, but they seem to have done a pretty decent job on you.'

Two months? What the hell had happened to him? His recollection was still hazy, but he caught a glimpse of himself at a window, a rifle in his hands ...

'You had a broken leg, two broken arms and a multitude of internal problems. I'm afraid your looks have gone, too.'

Gray's hands went to his face. 'Get me a mirror.'

Farrar handed one over and Gray examined himself. His hair was unkempt and at least three inches longer than he would have maintained it, and a moustache adorned his upper lip, while the rest of his face was clean-shaven.

But it was the shape of his face that shocked him.

His nose had been broken and was flattened across the middle of his face, and the top of his right ear was missing. A curved scar ran from the bottom of the ear down to the jaw line, and his brow jutted well over his eyes, giving him a Neanderthal appearance.

He looked like an old boxer: a very bad old boxer.

'What the fuck happened to me?'

'You had a particularly nasty accident which caused the scar and the small nick on the ear. The rest,' he smiled smugly, 'was all our work.'

'What? You did this to me? Why?'

'We did it because you would still have looked like Tom Gray, and I'm afraid Tom Gray is dead.'

He let the words sink in and was glad to see that Tom was struggling to handle the bombshell he had just dropped.

'I don't understand ... '

'No, I didn't think you'd be able to. After all, it isn't every day someone dies.'

Gray's head was swimming, and another glance in the mirror did him no favours.

'Is this hell?'

Farrar roared with laughter. 'Good Lord, no. Well, it depends on whether or not you like billions of mosquitoes and cockroaches the size of your dick. But no, you aren't dead. Tom Gray is, but you aren't.'

Perhaps it was the medication, he thought, but Gray just couldn't get his head around Farrar's cryptic comments. Farrar noticed the continuing confusion and decided to put him out of his misery.

'Your little escapade caused a lot of embarrassment to Her Majesty's government. When news first reached us about the explosion, there was utter panic, as you can imagine. Everyone thought you were dead, and a biological weapon was unaccounted for.

'Then we found out you were alive but barely able to breathe, never mind talk, so we concentrated our efforts on your colleagues.'

'What did you do to them? Where are they?'

'Relax, they are fine. In fact, you should be grateful to them. They refused to cooperate until the home secretary promised to honour the agreement, which he did, live on TV. It was only then that they revealed your little subterfuge, and that was a huge kick in the teeth for the security services, chasing their tails for days, looking for a bomb that never existed. The chumps at MI5 had taken a battering and wanted to come out of it smelling of roses, so they put out a statement to the press, saying the device had been made safe and no one was in any further danger.'

Farrar rubbed a handkerchief around his neck to soak up the sweat that was building, while mumbling something about the 'bloody humidity'.

'But why am I here? You said the home secretary honoured the agreement.'

'That's right, he did, and was all ready to jail you for life for the murder of Simon Arkin.'

'But Arkin wasn't dead,' Gray said. 'I mean, I didn't kill him. I remember that much.'

'Oh, we know that now, your friends told us right after the home secretary's TV announcement. The rescue services found evidence of the blood pack, but there wasn't enough of Simon left to establish a time of death. Therefore, you were going to face the murder charge and life in prison.'

'So what changed?'

'Your friends decided that, as free men, they would tell their story to the newspapers, and they stressed the *whole* story, unless the government admitted that Arkin died in the blast. They would mention the fact that there never was a bomb, contrary to what the security service had said, and that Simon Arkin was alive until the explosion killed him.'

'That still doesn't sound like a good enough reason to fake my death.'

'True, and it wasn't even considered at that point. But when half a million people brought London to a standstill for a fortnight protesting for your freedom, we came to a compromise: you disappear, new identity, new country; and they wouldn't go to the press.'

'Half a million people?' he said, amazed at the support he had gained.

'That was the conservative estimate. They camped out in the streets for thirteen days in all, and there were similar protests all over the country. Oh, and a seven-million-signature petition.'

'So why not just release me? Why the new identity?'

'Because you were becoming a hero, and there was the danger that you might continue the fight for a change in the law. We simply couldn't allow that to happen, so an announcement went out that you had died and you were whisked off to Farnborough.'

'Do I get a say in this?'

'Of course. You can go along with it and get a generous salary for the rest of your life, or,' and his demeanour changed instantly, 'you can tell the world that you're still alive, and we will happily remedy that within twenty-four hours.'

Gray yawned, despite the news he'd just received.

'I can see you're still tired,' Farrar said. 'We'll talk later.'

'But who attacked me? And what happened to the kids in the cells?' Gray asked, stifling another yawn.

'We've got plenty of time for all that, trust me. I'll give you all the details tomorrow, including your new role.'

'New role?'

'When you're on the payroll, you have to earn your money. I'll explain it all in the morning.'

Farrar clicked the button on the intravenous feed to dispense a little morphine and watched as Gray's eyes struggled to focus. After a minute they finally gave up the fight.

'Goodnight, Sam Grant.'